Hayes is fine with his life, no matter what his mother thinks. He's a mutant now, and he can't ignore that or the fact that the labs are still a reality — a reality he and the other mutants can change. There's no going back to his old life, and while the future feels complicated, Hayes is surrounded by friends and family and is proud of the work they do.

Rikar didn't hesitate to welcome the mutants into his tribe. The tribe has been rescuing people from the labs for decades, and the mutants have the same goals. Plus, they needed a home, and Rikar's small town has plenty of that.

When Rikar sees Hayes and realizes the mutant is his mate, he doesn't know what to do. Hayes is still dealing with the consequences of what was done to him in the lab, and Rikar leads a very large tribe.

But when Hayes crashes through Rikar's roof, Rikar can't avoid telling him about the bond that links them together. But as they try to work things out between them, Hayes and the mutants find a lab experimenting on children, and one of them latches onto Rikar.

Rikar wasn't prepared for a mate and a child. Hayes wasn't prepared for any of this. What are they supposed to do now?

Hayes
Copyright © 2022 Catherine Lievens
ISBN: 978-1-4874-3642-1
Cover art by Angela Waters

Published by eXtasy Books Inc

Look for us online at:
www.eXtasybooks.com

HAYES MUTANTS 2

BY

CATHERINE LIEVENS

CHAPTER ONE

The town was odd.

Hayes didn't think he'd ever been in such a place. Here, everyone was either part of the supernatural community or was somehow related to someone who was. Usually, they were mates, but there were also children, parents, and extended families.

Then there were the mutants.

No one had behaved strangely after the mutants had moved in. Hayes had expected some weird glances, maybe even insults. He wouldn't have been surprised, because that was how humans would have reacted to their presence. They wouldn't have trusted them because they were even more different than shifters.

Hell, Hayes wasn't even a shifter. He'd been human before, and he supposed that, in a way, he still was.

He was just a human who could fly now.

His phone vibrated on his nightstand, making him groan because he knew who was calling. His roommate and best friend, Jessup, chuckled from his bed.

"You know she'll call again," he said.

"I do know, but what am I supposed to tell her?"

"The usual—that you love her and that you'll visit soon."

Hayes scowled. "You *know* I won't."

"Why not? You still have a family, and they still want you. Do you know how rare that is?"

Hayes did. He understood where Jessup was coming from, but that didn't make it easier to deal with his mother. He'd

1

never had the guts to tell her exactly what had been done to him in that lab, even though he'd explained the consequences. He could never return to his old life, and she didn't understand that. She always tried to convince him to come home, return to his old job, and forget everything that happened, but Hayes couldn't do that.

Never again.

Sometimes he wished he'd gotten more than just being able to fly. It was useful, but being super strong would have been just as useful. He didn't feel he contributed much, but the other mutants insisted they wanted him with them for some reason.

So here he was.

His phone stopped vibrating. He and Jessup looked at each other, and Jessup raised his fingers. He counted down from five, and sure enough, as soon as the last finger was folded, the phone started vibrating again.

Jessup laughed, and Hayes threw him his pillow. He also grabbed the phone from his nightstand to answer.

"Hey, Mom," he said.

"You didn't answer before," were her first words.

"Hello to you, too. Why, yes, I'm fine. What about you?"

She huffed. "All right, all right. I realize I was rude, and I apologize. So, how are you? Why didn't you answer before?"

"I was in the bathroom."

Jessup grinned from the other side of the room and threw the pillow back at Hayes, who caught it, bundled it up, and pushed it under his head. He stared at the ceiling, and while part of him missed his mom and his family, the other part knew that no matter how much he wished he did, he didn't belong with them anymore.

"I'm sorry," his mom said, and she indeed sounded sorry. "I'm just worried."

Hayes didn't blame her. After all, he'd been kidnapped

and had disappeared for months. His family had looked for him everywhere, but there hadn't been any traces of him. Even the authorities hadn't been able to do anything, and for good reason since he'd been locked in a lab, being experimented on until something in him changed. Flying was in his DNA now.

"I know, and you don't have anything to worry about," Hayes said.

"How am I supposed to know that when I never see you?"

"I'm busy."

"Too busy to visit your family?"

Hayes gritted his teeth. He *did* understand where his mom was coming from and why she needed to see him. Even though he was safe and had been safe for months now, he'd only visited a few times. He didn't feel like he could go more often, but it had nothing to do with his family and everything to do with himself.

He didn't belong anymore. He might still be human, but not entirely, and the fact that his mother tried her hardest to act as if that wasn't the case didn't help. She believed that as long as Hayes *wanted* everything to go back to normal and to forget what happened to him, he could.

There was nothing further from the truth.

No matter how much Hayes loved his family, he couldn't return to his old life. The other mutants knew what he'd been through, and even though they weren't related by blood, they were connected through their experiences. Hayes felt like they were the only ones who could truly understand how he felt and accept him, no matter what his mother believed.

"You know what I do," he said, staring at the ceiling.

"I do, and it makes me even more worried. You shouldn't be running around attacking people. What will happen if someone finds out about all of this?"

"You make me sound like a serial killer," Hayes grumbled.

His mother sucked in a breath. "Please tell me you haven't killed anyone."

"Of course not. You know that what I can do isn't useful in a fight. I almost never have to get physical."

She made a small sound, maybe of dismay. It was hard to read her on the phone. "What you can do is . . . special, but it doesn't mean you should use it."

"Can we not talk about this right now?" Because Hayes already knew how it would end, and he wasn't up for that. "We have a meeting, so I better go."

"Wait," his mother protested. "Why don't you come to dinner?"

Hayes's first instinct was to say no, but not only would it hurt his mother, it would also give her a reason to call again. She'd continue doing so until he said yes and went, and once again, it would be easier for him just to give in now.

He sighed, trying to ignore Jessup was grinning like an idiot. "When?"

"You can come whenever you want."

"That doesn't help me much, Mom. I'll tell you what, why don't you text me when you think would be a good evening for me to come around? I know you'll want to call Lucas and find out if he can come, too, and with his job, it's better if you make sure he's available, right? Just let me know, and I'll tell you if I can or can't come."

"All right, but you *will* come this time."

"It's not my fault I had to cancel the last time."

His mom sniffed. "You were on a mission. You already told me that."

"I also apologized."

"I know." Her voice softened. "I just worry."

"You don't have to. I'm not a child anymore, and I'm safe."

"You'll always be my baby."

Hayes groaned. "Don't start calling me that."

Jessup guffawed. Hayes flipped him the bird, and Jessup got to his feet. He stretched, and Hayes wondered what he was about to do. Then Jessup moved toward him and grabbed his hand.

"We have to go," he said loud enough that Hayes's mom could hear him.

Hayes could have kissed him, but that would have been weird, because Jessup was like another brother.

"Hear that?" he asked his mother. "I have to go."

"Be careful, will you?"

"I'm always careful."

"Yet we both know what happened."

Hayes cringed, but his mother didn't have anything else to say about that. She still had a hard time wrapping her mind around the fact that he'd been kidnapped and held in a lab. It was something that happened to others, not to her son.

But Hayes *had* been kidnapped, and he'd been experimented on. He'd been changed, and no matter how easy it was for his mother to ignore that fact, he couldn't. The fact that he wasn't fully human anymore was part of his life, and she did need to accept that, just like he had.

And she would, just as soon as pigs grew wings.

Rikar checked his reflection in the mirror. He looked good, or at least good enough for dinner with his mothers. They'd probably have something to say about his appearance anyway, and the thought made him smile. He might be the leader of his tribe, and he might have rescued more people than he could remember, but to his mothers, he'd always be the child who couldn't tie his shoes until he was ten.

Since what he looked like didn't matter, he stepped away from the mirror and turned to grab his cell phone and keys. He looked around his little house one last time, trying to find a reason to cancel dinner. He loved his mothers, and they loved him, but sometimes they could be a lot.

That was especially true when it came to him being the leader. Most tribe members were more than happy to let him take the lead, which was right since they'd wanted him to be in charge. Rikar's mothers always had something to say about his decisions, though. They still viewed him as their little boy, and while sometimes it was amusing, other times it was irritating. Rikar had no doubt that tonight they'd want to know about the mutants, and he wasn't sure what to tell them.

Yes, they were different, and yes, they might be dangerous. Rikar didn't think so, though, which was why he'd been willing to give them a chance. They needed a home, a place where they could be safe and where they'd know that no one would attack them. Considering what most of them went through, Rikar had felt it necessary to welcome them. He realized that not everyone in the tribe was okay with that, but most of the people who lived here had been in a lab at one time or another. They knew what the mutants had gone through, and Rikar had every hope that eventually everyone would get used to their presence and the mutants would truly become part of the tribe.

They weren't for now. They lived in town, but they weren't tribe members. They didn't answer to Rikar, but rather to their leader, Moore. That was fine with Rikar. He already had more than enough people to give him headaches every day.

He locked his door, even though nothing ever happened in their small town. It was made up of the tribe in which Rikar was born, and of course of some of the people he and the tribe had rescued over the years. They'd been doing this job for decades, and most of those people had become tribe members. The tribe had so many members now that their village was a small town, and Rikar was the unofficial mayor.

He walked down Main Street, nodding at some of the

people he crossed paths with on the sidewalk. They nodded back, smiled at him, and a little girl ran to him to wrap herself around his legs. He patted her head and beamed, happy in a way he'd never thought he could be.

But he was.

No matter how complicated things were, this was his home and the home to other people who needed a place to feel safe. He was more than happy to provide them with that.

He could see the diner where he usually met his mothers. The lights blazed, illuminating the street in front of it, and when the door opened to let a couple out, he could smell sizzling meat and home-made pies.

His stomach rumbled.

The air was cooling as the evening settled in, and he was more than happy to walk into the diner. He turned to the right, smiling when he saw his mothers were already there.

Not that he'd doubted they would be.

They were talking. The way they were speaking made Rikar wonder if something was happening, but they both looked up when he got closer and smiled.

Blodwyn's smile was a bit tense, and the first thing that came out of her mouth was, "I'm sorry."

That was when Rikar noticed the man sitting at the table, almost plastered against the wall. Blodwyn sat in front of him while Rikar's other mother was next to him.

He was a Nix, just like the three of them. Rikar was pretty sure he was a tribe member, but with the tribe growing so quickly and so much, he didn't know all of the members personally. He racked his brain, trying to remember the man's name, but he didn't have to worry, because his other mother, Elna, got to her feet.

"You're finally here," she scolded. "We were getting worried. Sit down, sit down."

Rikar shrugged off his jacket and dropped it by the

window. Elna wrinkled her nose, but thankfully, she didn't say anything about that. Rikar was an adult and didn't need to be scolded for how he treated his clothes.

Blodwyn got to her feet to let him sit, and Elna settled back down next to the man, who was staring at Rikar with wide eyes.

"What's going on?" Rikar asked.

Blodwyn looked like she wished to be anywhere but here, so Rikar suspected she had nothing to do with whatever was happening. Elna, on the other hand, was right in the middle of it.

"We brought you a date," she announced.

Rikar stared at her for a moment before groaning. "What? *Why?*"

Elna wasn't offended. "Because you need someone in your life," she explained. She reached down and patted the hand of the poor man she'd convinced to come. "And Kamrey would be perfect for you."

The name wasn't familiar, which told Rikar that he'd probably never spoken to Kamrey. "I thought I told you I didn't need you to help me find dates," he said through gritted teeth.

He loved his mothers, but Elna could be a lot sometimes.

Hell, most of the time.

She meant well. She wanted him to be happy and thought that would happen if he found someone to share his life with. She might be right, but he had no intention of finding out if Kamrey could make him happy. The man looked sweet, but Rikar had no intention of becoming close to him or anyone else. His life was as complicated as he could take it at the moment.

He forced himself to smile, because none of this was Kamrey's fault.

"It's a pleasure to meet you," he said. "And I'm sorry you were dragged into this."

Kamrey looked from Rikar to Elna. "I thought you knew."

"Neither of my mothers told me anything about your presence here tonight. I believed I would be eating dinner with them, not having a blind date."

Kamrey's cheeks flushed. "I'm really sorry. I didn't know anything about this."

"I don't blame you. My mother could convince Satan to kiss children. I'm just sorry you were involved. I'm not looking for a relationship, and I hate that you wasted your time."

Elna sucked in a breath. "Don't be rude," she protested.

"I'm not being rude. I'm just being honest, which you should have been from the beginning."

"We want you to be happy."

"And is it so hard to believe that I already am?"

"I believe your mother is trying to say that we'd like for you to have a family," Blodwyn intervened. "We know you're happy as our tribe leader and that you feel your life is full, and we'd never assume to know better than you, but would it be so bad to have someone to go home to at night?"

It took everything Rikar had not to leave. He didn't want to fight with his mothers. They might have gone about it wrong, but they just wanted his happiness. They loved him, and he loved them, and in the end, that was what mattered the most.

Rikar sighed. "Fine. I'll have dinner with the three of you, but that's it."

Elna got to her feet so fast that Rikar wouldn't have been surprised if she'd flipped the table. "Actually, Blodwyn and I have something else to do. It's an emergency, and we're sorry we couldn't tell you before."

Rikar wasn't even surprised. "An emergency?"

Elna nodded. "Yes. We'll see you tomorrow, all right?"

They were out of the diner so fast that Rikar couldn't even agree. He watched them power-walk to the door, torn between the need to go after them and the unwillingness to leave poor Kamrey alone.

He sighed. Well, he supposed that at least he wouldn't be having dinner on his own.

Hayes looked up at the sound of the diner door opening and closing again. He let his gaze wander for a moment, still not quite able to believe he was really here, having dinner with his closest friends. There had been a time when he'd thought he'd lost all of this, that he'd lost *life*. He'd wanted to die when he was in the lab, and while now he was glad he hadn't, he'd come close a few times. But he was free, and he had every intention of clinging to life for as long as he could.

His gaze caught on a blond man sitting at the table in the back. He wasn't alone, but Hayes barely looked at the other guy. They were similar, with blond hair, pointed ears, and from what he could see, light-colored eyes. Only one of them held his attention, though.

As with shifters, it was almost impossible to tell how old the Nix was. At first glance, he appeared to be in his early, possibly mid-thirties. He could be anywhere from that age to seventy, so Hayes couldn't be sure.

And why couldn't he look away?

He wasn't sure what it was about this man. He'd met plenty of Nix before, yet none of them had caught his attention the way this guy was. It was so bad that Hayes wondered what would happen if he got to his feet and headed over there.

The only reason he didn't was that he was pretty sure the guy was on a date. The other man at the table was visibly flustered. His cheeks were flushed, and he spoke quickly, his hands waving around as he did so. The man Hayes wanted to spread out on one of the tables and have his way with smiled, then nodded, and the other guy relaxed.

For some reason, Hayes didn't like him.

That wasn't like him. He didn't usually dislike people, and when he did, there was a good reason for that. He didn't even know this guy's name, so why did he feel like he wanted to go over there and drag him away?

"What are you staring at?" Jessup said, startling Hayes.

"Nothing," Hayes hurried to say.

But Jessup had caught him. "Which one?" he asked, wiggling his eyebrows up and down. "Rikar or the other one?"

Hayes frowned. "Which one is Rikar?"

"You don't know the leader of the tribe we live with?"

Hayes glared at him. "I might have heard Moore mention that name, but I had no idea it was that guy." So Hayes had been staring at the tribe leader. That could become a problem if the guy caught him, but so far, he was focused on the man eating with him.

The man Hayes wanted to kick out of the diner.

"Hayes?" Jessup asked. He was frowning now, too, and clearly worried.

Hayes wondered if he'd missed something Jessup had said, but he had no idea and wasn't about to ask. "Well, I didn't know that was the tribe leader," he said.

"And that's okay. Something's happening, though."

"I'm perfectly fine."

Jessup didn't look convinced. "You know you can talk to me, right?"

Hayes forced himself to relax. What was happening to him? Why was he reacting this way to a guy he'd never even talked to? He didn't like feeling out of control, and that was how Rikar made him feel. He didn't care why that was. The only thing he cared about was that he wanted to stay as far away from Rikar as possible, yet at the same time, he also wanted to wrap himself around him.

11

Something was *definitely* wrong with him.

He shook his head. "I'm fine. Just distracted, I guess."

"What is it? Your mom?"

Hayes didn't want to talk about her, but he supposed that was better than talking about his weird obsession with Rikar. "She still thinks I can forget all of this and go back to what she calls a normal life."

Jessup grimaced. "I can understand why you've been reluctant to go home. Does she talk about that every time you visit?"

"Basically. I understand why she feels that way and wants to forget everything she's gone through, but I can't. I can't ignore what was done to me."

Jessup patted Hayes's hand. "I know. No one expects you to forget all about that."

Hayes snorted. "No one except my mother."

"She doesn't understand, but we do. I'm sure she'll eventually stop trying to convince you."

"I wouldn't be too sure about that." Because Hayes's mom was stubborn.

He wouldn't be surprised if she had something up her sleeve and her invitation for him to go to dinner was a ruse. He wasn't afraid for his safety, but he was afraid for his sanity. His mom could drive him nuts like no one else could, even though she only wanted the best for him, or maybe because of that.

She believed the best for Hayes was to go back to his old life, forget that he'd been kidnapped and experimented on, and focus on his future. She didn't understand that was what he was doing, just not the way she thought he should do it.

"She'll understand eventually," Jessup murmured.

Hayes hoped she would.

His gaze drifted back to Rikar. Now that he knew who he was, he thought he remembered seeing him around. He and the others hadn't spent much time away from their new homes, but they'd gone to the stores to buy some of the things they'd missed while squatting in abandoned buildings. Having a home was a huge change for the better. If they were here, it was all thanks to Rikar, and Hayes wondered why the man had agreed to let them stay. He hadn't known them. He'd just known they were in need of a place to call home, and he'd provided it to them.

Knowing that made Hayes like him even more, which wasn't something he needed. He seemed to already be obsessed with the guy, so he forced himself to look away and back to Jessup and their friends.

After Hayes had hung up with his mother, Jessup had dragged him downstairs. There, they'd found several others hanging around, spread out on the couches relaxing. It wasn't something they'd had many opportunities to do when they'd been living on their own, and now, everyone was taking advantage of the fact that they were safe.

So Jessup had gathered a small group of them, and they'd walked to the diner. He'd been leaving the house more often than the others, and he'd been getting to know the people who lived in town. He was more outgoing than Hayes could ever hope to be, but that was fine. Hayes didn't need friends when he already had his mutant family.

"We should head out," Olga said as she got to her feet.

She had that weird expression she usually sported when she knew something was about to happen. Her power was clairvoyance, and while she always said that it wasn't precise and that many things changed in as little as a second, she knew things. It was clear she'd seen something about to happen, so Hayes quickly got up. Whatever it was, he trusted Olga, and if she said they needed to leave, then that was what they should do.

"Rikar is a nice guy," she said as Hayes came to stand next

to her.

He blinked at her. "I'm sure he is."

She grinned. "Just saying."

"I get that."

"So don't freak out, all right?"

"What are you talking about?"

She patted Hayes's shoulder. "Nothing."

He groaned. "You know I hate when you're all mysterious and shit."

She laughed, loud enough that several people turned to look at her. "Most people hate it when I'm like this, but what fun would this power of mine be if I couldn't do this?"

Hayes supposed she wasn't wrong. In a physical fight, she wouldn't be much help, just like he wouldn't. They both trained with the others, but their powers weren't aimed for offense. No, her role came before the fights happened. Even though everyone knew that her power wasn't precise, they trusted her enough to follow her lead when she said so.

So when she walked toward the door, Hayes followed. That meant he couldn't back down when he realized that she wasn't headed for the exit. No, she was headed for the table where Rikar and his date were sitting.

Rikar looked up when he felt someone stop next to him. Olga, Moore's second, beamed at Rikar. For a moment, he was confused. It would make sense for her to stop and say hello, but why did she seem so happy to see him?

The next moment, Rikar forgot all about Olga and her reason for being there, because his gaze crossed with the gaze of the man standing next to her. Rikar was pretty sure he was one of Olga's mutants, which would make sense, since the mutants tended to stick together. They'd been here to have dinner, just like Rikar.

That wasn't what caught Rikar's attention. No, it was the fact that this man, whoever he was, was Rikar's mate.

Rikar's mouth went dry. He wanted to burst out crying and laughing at the same time. He wanted to tell this man they were mates and shout it from the rooftops. He wanted to take the man's hand and pull him close, and he almost did, but he caught himself in time.

The last thing he should do was to make his mate freak out.

"We thought we'd stop to say hello," Olga said. "This is Hayes,"

Rikar swallowed, trying to find his voice. The first thing that came out was a croak, so he tried again, clearing his throat. "It's a pleasure to meet you," he said.

Hayes nodded. He seemed to have trouble looking away from Rikar, which Rikar fully understood, because he was having the same problem.

"It truly is," Hayes said. He looked from Rikar to Kamrey. "But we should probably leave you to your date."

"No!" Rikar yelled.

Everyone around him froze except for Olga, who was grinning like a loon. That was when Rikar remembered that she had the power of clairvoyance. From her expression, she'd known what would happen if she introduced Hayes and Rikar.

Rikar narrowed his eyes at her. Her smile widened, and that was all the reaction she gave him. She wasn't going to interfere, which meant Rikar was on his own, which was just as good.

The problem was that he didn't know what to do. Should he tell Hayes they were mates? He knew Hayes wasn't a Nix, and not just because he didn't have pointed ears and blond hair. He hadn't reacted to Rikar's presence, which meant he hadn't recognized him as his mate. That meant he was either human or a shifter, but a shifter might have already smelled

Rikar.

That left human.

Knowing what he did about the mutants and what had happened to them, Rikar wasn't sure that blurting out that they were mates in the middle of the diner, in front of Hayes's friend, was a good idea. He desperately wanted to, but instead, he cleared his throat again. "I apologize. But you're welcome to sit with us."

Hayes shook his head. "We already had dinner. I'll see you around, though."

Rikar nodded. "Of course. I look forward to having the time to talk to you."

Hayes looked a bit puzzled but pleased as he turned around. Olga winked at Rikar, then followed Hayes, and their little group left the diner. Rikar couldn't look away and watched Hayes walk down the sidewalk, leaning close to one of his friends.

Or were they more than friends?

"Rikar?" Kamrey asked softly.

Rikar felt guilty, because he'd almost forgotten Kamrey was here. He'd been clear that this wasn't a date and that he didn't expect the two of them to end up together, but he'd still promised Kamrey a friendly dinner. One could never have too many friends, especially as a tribe leader.

Rikar sat back down. "Sorry about that."

"It's fine." Kamrey's smile was hesitant. "But something happened there."

Rikar swallowed heavily and nodded. "Something did. Look, I'm sorry my mother dragged you into this. She never should have, because I wasn't looking for a date."

Kamrey cocked his head. "You said *wasn't*. Has that changed?"

"No. I'm still not looking for a date." Not when he'd just met his mate. The only dates he'd have in the future were the ones he and Hayes would go on, but Rikar didn't know where to start. He hadn't expected to meet his mate tonight or to realize that his mate had been living in town for several weeks.

Rikar had told himself he'd eventually meet all the mutants and that maybe he should organize a dinner to get to know them, but he hadn't gotten around to doing it yet. Now he realized he should have, but the past was the past, and there was nothing he could do to change it.

But he *could* mold the future.

"Rikar?" Kamrey gently pushed. "I understand you didn't expect this to be a date, but I thought that maybe we could still try to see if things can work between us? I mean, we're here."

"I'm sorry." Rikar wanted to let Kamrey down as gently as possible. "But I've met my mate."

Kamrey's eyes widened. "You have? When? Why didn't you tell me before?"

"I would have if I'd met them before, but you just saw our first meeting."

Kamrey frowned. "Olga?"

Rikar had believed his fascination with Hayes was obvious, but maybe he'd been hiding his feelings better than he'd expected. "No. Hayes."

Kamrey's smile disappeared. "I should have expected it. He's a gorgeous man."

"That's not why I want him." Although Rikar couldn't deny Hayes was gorgeous. From his appearance, he had to be a few years younger than Rikar, if he was human. Rikar wasn't sure about that, but he suspected it. Hayes's brown hair was cut short, and his brown eyes had been confused but warm. He wasn't very tall, and his body had looked solid under his clothes.

Thinking of him made Rikar want to leave Kamrey and go after him, but he forced himself to stay where he was. He didn't know anything about Hayes, and the last thing he wanted was to scare him. That wouldn't be the best way for them to start a relationship.

"I know it's not," Kamrey said softly. "I'm happy for you. It's always a good thing when a Nix meets his mate. I guess I just hoped that the two of us would work."

"We wouldn't have even if I hadn't met Hayes," Rikar explained. "My mothers mean well, but they don't understand that I didn't want anyone."

"But now you want Hayes."

Rikar nodded. He hadn't been looking for a relationship, mostly because he didn't have time for one. Being the leader of so many people was a full-time job, and by the time he was done with his day, he barely had the energy to eat something and drag himself into bed. He had no idea how he'd fit Hayes into that life, but he supposed he was about to find out.

"Even though things can't work between us, we could still be friends," he offered.

Kamrey's smile turned a bit more natural. "I'd like that. I never expected I'd be the leader's friend, but I can't say I hate the idea."

Rikar grinned. "As long as you tell my mothers that I'm not your kind of guy and that it was a disaster, we can be friends."

Kamrey laughed. "I wouldn't go so far as to say it's a disaster, but I'll tell her that we work better as friends." He hesitated. "Won't you tell them that you met your mate?"

Rikar rubbed his forehead. "Eventually I will. But things with Hayes might be a bit complicated. I'm pretty sure he's human, and of course, he's one of the mutants. He's gone through a lot, and I don't want to push him in a direction he's not ready to take or send him running."

Kamrey patted Rikar's hand on the table. "You'll find a way to make it work. I have faith in you."

That was good, because Rikar didn't have a lot of faith in

himself. He was a leader, yet he had no idea where to start when it came to Hayes. His only hope was that Hayes would eventually come to feel the mate bond between them. As a human, he might not be able to identify it, but he'd realize what it meant.

Hopefully it would be as important to him as it was to Rikar. Rikar had never wished to have the same power as Olga, but right now, he did. He wanted to know whether or not he and Hayes would be together.

More importantly, he wanted to know if they'd be happy.

Chapter Two

Olga kept staring at Hayes. That was enough to tell him something was up, but she refused to answer when he asked. It was irritating, and Hayes had made sure to tell her. He also glared at her every time she stared at him like that, but she wasn't offended. If anything, she seemed even more amused.

Hayes wasn't.

She was staring at him from the other side of the living room. Moore and his mate, Jolyn, were sitting next to her on the couch, and the three were talking. Every so often, they looked at Hayes in a way that made Hayes think they knew what Olga was hiding.

But *he* didn't, even though it was clear it involved him.

He glared at them and turned back to his phone. He'd promised his mother he'd go over for dinner, and she'd given him several days from which he could choose, but he still hadn't. It wasn't that he didn't want to visit her and the rest of the family. He did want to, and he missed them. He was just afraid of what would happen when he got there.

His mother couldn't understand. No one but the other mutants and council assassins could. Hayes would never tell his mother, father, or brother what had been done to him. They knew what the result was, but that was it. Hayes never wanted to think about the lab again, and telling his family would only make things worse, because his mother would freak out and try to protect him even more, which was the last thing he needed.

"Why is Olga staring at you?" Jessup asked as he flopped onto the couch next to Hayes.

The house wasn't huge, but it was big enough for several of them to live there. Hayes and Jessup shared a room, as well as Hansen and Teddy, and Elsa and Sophie. The other mutants lived in different homes, but they were all in each other's pockets. They were used to it, especially their little core group. It meant they visited each other's places and were together more often than not, which was what had happened today.

But that didn't explain why Olga was staring.

Hayes huffed. "She's been doing that since that night at the diner, and she won't tell me what happened."

Jessup wrinkled his nose. "Probably nothing for now. I mean, she sees what's going to happen, right?" He rolled his head on the back of the couch to look at Hayes. "Do you think it's a good thing?"

Hayes couldn't know for sure, but from the way Olga stared, he suspected it was. There was always a smile playing on her lips when she stared, and she'd winked at him a few times.

"Hayes, when's the last time you trained?" she suddenly asked.

Everyone's attention turned to Hayes. He had no idea where this question was coming from, but from Olga's expression, he could tell she knew what she was doing.

"It's been a while," he admitted. "With everything that happened, finding time hasn't been easy."

Moore snorted. "That's bullshit. We've been living here for a while now. While I understand that all of you wanted to get used to this and to have a home again, we can't afford *not* to train."

Hayes looked away, properly chastised. He knew they were right. If he wanted to be of any use, he needed to control his flying ability, which wasn't the case at the moment.

People in movies made flying look easy, but there was nothing further from the truth. When Hayes was in the air, his balance was completely off. He had to move his body differently to do the same things he did while his feet were on the ground, and it was confusing, if not impossible to understand sometimes.

So yes, he needed to train and to be able to control his ability so that the next time they entered a lab, he would be of better use.

He sighed. "You're right. I'll train as soon as possible."

Olga's eyes twinkled. "You should go now. Take Leon with you, maybe?"

Hayes raised an eyebrow. "Why? You think I'm going to fall?" Leon's ability was healing, very much like a Nix's. He'd told Hayes that his ability was even better because it was easier for him to heal, but Hayes wouldn't know about that. He had no idea how it worked or how a Nix's healing worked.

"I never said that."

"So you know I'm going to fall."

She chuckled. "Again, I never said that. Just go. Find Leon and take him to the park just off Main Street. There, you'll be able to train without anyone bothering you."

The place wasn't exactly a park, no matter what Olga called it. It was a patch of green in the middle of town, and sure, there were trees and grass, but it had been left wild. Hayes had seen children play there, but he wouldn't qualify it as a park. Still, it would probably be empty at this time of day, since kids were in school, and it should be safe enough for him to train there.

He got to his feet, still wondering what Olga was seeing about him that made her behave the way she did. "You can't continue to do that," he warned her.

She batted her eyelashes and pushed her dark hair from

her face. "Do what?"

Hayes rolled his eyes. "Sure. Play innocent. We both know that's not true."

This time Olga outright laughed. "I'm far from being innocent. And I know I'm bothering you, but just go along with it for a bit longer, all right? I could tell you what I saw, but there would be a good chance that it wouldn't happen if I did, and I don't want things to go that way." Her expression became more serious. "You don't know how hard it is to deal with this ability. I'm happy to explain things when they mean that I can keep everyone safe, but I decided not to talk about the other things I see. It wouldn't be fair to any of you, and it might change the future, which isn't something I want to do."

Hayes got to his feet and went to crouch in front of her. They were a family, and no matter how annoyed Hayes was with Olga, he never wanted to make her unhappy. "I might not understand what it's like to have your power, but if you don't want me to continue asking, I won't."

She laughed again. "Oh, I love teasing you about this. Just keep in mind I won't tell you anything."

Hayes grinned. "And here I was trying to be nice."

Olga patted his cheek. "You *are* nice. Just go, all right?"

"I will." There was a certain urgency in Olga's voice, and it was enough to push Hayes to go right away. He waved at the people gathered in the living room, grabbed his cell phone, put his shoes on, and left the house.

Luckily, Leon and some others lived right next door, so Hayes didn't have to go far. He climbed down the porch steps, walked over, then climbed up more steps. The door opened before he could knock, and Leon stood there.

He grinned when he saw Hayes's surprise and raised his phone. "Olga texted."

Hayes sighed. "Of course she did. Well? Want to come with me and train?"

"You think you're going to need my ability?" Leon asked as he stepped out of the house and closed the door. They were both wearing light jackets because, while the weather was cooling, it was still nice enough for them not to have to dress warmly. It was nice to know that even once the weather turned cold, they wouldn't be in as much trouble as they'd been last year. They wouldn't be squatting. Instead, they'd be living in warm homes, so they wouldn't get sick.

They were safe now, even though it was hard to wrap his mind around some days.

"I hope I won't need you, but if Olga says you have to come with me, then you have to come with me," Hayes told Leon.

Leon nodded. "Then let's go."

Hayes wasn't particularly looking forward to having to fly, but he followed Leon toward the park. This needed to be done, and the sooner he did it, the sooner he could stop doing it.

He didn't hate his ability, but it puzzled him, and he didn't understand how it worked. He supposed he didn't have to in order to make it work, though, so, as soon as he and Leon were in the park far away from anyone Hayes might hurt, Hayes pushed into the air.

There was nothing exhilarating about flying, especially since Hayes had always been afraid of heights. He lost his balance when he was in the air and took a few seconds to tighten his abdominal muscles and try to keep it up. Once he was sure he had it, he opened his eyes to find Leon staring at him and giving him a thumbs up.

"Show me what you can do!" Leon exclaimed.

Hayes grinned at him and did just that.

"Keep an eye open, all right?" Rikar said.

Cyrus chuckled. "When have I not kept an eye open?"

That much was true. They were allies, and Cyrus and his people had helped Rikar several times when he'd liberated a lab. Cyrus had taken in some of the people who didn't want to stay with the tribe, and they lived not far away, allies and friends like always. "I apologize," Rikar told him.

"Don't. I know you're under some stress." Cyrus hesitated. "How is it with those mutants?"

"I don't know what you've heard, but they haven't caused me any kind of problem."

"I never said they had. I just imagine that things are odd right now. It's a bunch of new people to get used to living with."

Rikar was on the defensive when it came to the mutants, and it wasn't hard to understand why. "What have you heard?"

"Nothing bad, I promise. But I have to say I was shocked when I found out that you'd taken them in. Not many people would have."

"And I'm not like many people."

Cyrus laughed. "That much is true. Well, as long as they're not giving you problems, I'm sure they'll be an asset to the tribe."

"And to our mission."

Cyrus made a disgusted sound. "I can't believe that after all these years, we still have to go out and deal with those labs. Didn't they hurt us enough?"

Rikar didn't know what to say. When shifters had come out to the world, he, like many others, had hoped it meant that the humans would stop experimenting on them. They should have known better. Instead of stopping, they'd gone underground, which made it harder to find them. But it was the job Rikar had given himself, and he had every intention of doing it, no matter what happened. The people who were still in the labs deserved his help.

Like always when he focused on the labs, his thoughts drifted to Hayes. When he thought about what had probably been done to Hayes, he wanted to hit something, preferably the people who'd hurt him. They hadn't even talked, yet here he was, wanting to go out there and avenge his mate. It was ridiculous, but not unexpected.

The sound of something heavy crashing into Rikar's living room made him jump. It was so loud that Cyrus heard it, too. "What was that?" he asked.

"I have no idea. It came from my living room."

"Is the town under attack?"

Rikar stepped away from his kitchen counter and headed to the door. "I don't think so." Whatever it was had stopped, and he couldn't hear anything from the living room.

"Do you need me to send people?"

"I'll be fine," he promised. "It's probably the kids playing around or something. I'll call you back, all right?"

"Maybe we should stay on the phone until you're sure everything is fine."

The words made Rikar smile. He might be an only child, but it didn't mean he didn't have a family and siblings. Cyrus was one of the people he was closest to, and he'd come running if Rikar asked him.

Rikar didn't need to.

He peeked into the living room, unsure what to expect, and his eyes widened. There was a hole in the roof, and on the floor, in the middle of debris and bits of wood, was Hayes lying flat on his back.

Rikar stared for a second. Then, never looking away, he told Cyrus. "I'll call you back. Everything's fine. Someone just crashed through my roof."

"What the fuck does that mean?"

"I promise I'll explain everything, but I need to check that Hayes is fine."

Cyrus was still protesting by the time Rikar hung up the phone. He put it on the small table in the entrance, then stepped into the living room.

Hayes groaned and raised a hand.

At least he wasn't unconscious.

Hayes rubbed his forehead, then blinked his eyes open and stared at the hole over him. "Shit," he muttered. Finally he sat up.

Since he seemed to be all right, Rikar gave himself permission to relax. He leaned his shoulder against the doorframe, crossed his arms over his chest, and took a moment to watch Hayes, who still hadn't realized he was there.

Rikar had no idea how Hayes had ended up falling through his roof, but he couldn't say he minded. He'd been trying to find a way to get to Hayes, but so far, the only thing he'd been able to think of was to go up to the house and knock on the door, which might not be the best idea.

Or maybe it was, but even if so, now Hayes was in Rikar's living room, and Rikar would make the most of it.

"Care to tell me what happened?" he drawled.

Hayes jerked and started scrambling away, but then he realized who was talking to him and froze. He stared at Rikar with wide eyes, and Rikar stared back.

"What are you doing here?" Hayes eventually asked.

"I feel I should be the one asking that." Rikar approached from the doorframe and stepped into the living room.

He looked up at the hole. There wasn't a Hayes shape in it, but there might as well be. The hole was big enough that someone could crawl into the house through it, and Rikar could see the sky. Thankfully, Hayes had managed to avoid the thick wooden beams, because if he hadn't, he'd be hurt, but as it was, Rikar would need someone to come and fix the roof.

"Shit," Hayes murmured. "Is this your place?"

Rikar nodded. "It is. I have to admit I'm curious about why you fell through my roof."

Hayes was still on the floor, which was starting to worry Rikar. He moved closer and knelt next to Hayes, reaching for him without meaning to. He needed to ensure that his mate was okay, and Hayes watched him with wide eyes as Rikar cupped a hand on the back of his head and felt around for wounds or bumps.

"What are you doing?" Hayes asked.

The blush on Hayes's cheeks made Rikar want to lean in and kiss him. He suspected that would freak Hayes out even more, so he kept his lips to himself and focused on what he was doing. "Making sure you're fine."

"I promise I am."

"Maybe, but I need to check you on my own."

Hayes blinked. "Why?"

Rikar hesitated. It would be easier for him to explain that Hayes was his mate, but was this the right moment?

He'd been thinking about how and when to tell Hayes, and while he wanted it to be perfect, he already knew it wouldn't be. There would never be a perfect moment for them to talk about this, and the longer Rikar waited, the worse it would be. Hayes deserved to know what they were to each other, and it wasn't fair of Rikar to keep that information to himself.

He dropped his hand to one of his knees. "How are you feeling?"

"I told you that I'm fine. Actually, I should probably go."

Rikar raised a hand. "Don't."

Hayes looked guilty. "I swear I'll fix the roof."

"You need to see a healer. You could be hurt."

"My friend is outside, and he'll make sure I'm not."

Hayes was trying to run away, but Rikar couldn't let him without telling him what was between them. So he caught one of his hands and pulled him back down to the floor. Hayes's eyes widened, and he tensed as if he expected Rikar to hit him for what he'd done.

Instead, Rikar looked him in the eyes and explained, "You're my mate."

Hayes stared. That was all he did, but Rikar wasn't offended. He'd been in shock when he'd realized that Hayes was his mate back at the diner, and now it was Hayes's turn to feel that way. Telling Hayes was the right thing to do, but Rikar couldn't help but wonder how Hayes would react. Would he want him? Would he be willing to give their bond a chance? Or would he freak out and run away? Rikar wouldn't blame him if that was what he did, but he hoped that wouldn't be the case. He couldn't say he was in love with his mate yet, but eventually, he would be.

But only if both of them gave their relationship a chance.

Hayes couldn't do anything but stare. What was he supposed to say about that? What was he supposed to do?

His brain scrambled to catch up with what Rikar had said, but it was stuck.

You're my mate.

That was what Rikar had said, and Hayes wondered if he'd heard it right. He had to have, because what else could Rikar have said? There was no denying those words, but what did they mean? Were they the truth, or was Rikar getting revenge for the hole Hayes had made in his roof?

"Hayes?" a voice called from outside. Leon sounded worried, which made sense, considering he'd just watched Hayes crash through Rikar's roof.

Hayes didn't look away from Rikar. He licked his lips, knowing he needed to reassure Leon but unable to do so.

"Is this your friend who was waiting for you outside?" Rikar asked.

Hayes nodded. "Olga told me to take him with me. It was

almost as if she knew I'd crash through your roof." She probably had, and while Hayes understood why she hadn't told him, he'd have appreciated the heads up. This wasn't the best way to make a good impression on Rikar and seduce him.

Not that Hayes had been planning on seducing him when he'd crashed through the roof.

"Hayes?" Leon called out again.

Rikar got to his feet. Hayes scrambled to follow him, but Rikar pointed at the couch. It was dusty, and a piece of wood lay on it, but Rikar brushed that to the floor, then pointed at the couch again. "Sit down."

"I should go," Hayes said, even though it was the last thing he wanted to do.

"You'll be allowed to as soon as I'm sure you're all right."

Hayes narrowed his eyes. "Allowed to?"

But Rikar was already gone. Hayes heard him walk away, then a door opened. Apparently, Rikar was reassuring Leon that Hayes was okay.

Hayes buried his face in his hands. What the fuck had he done?

He'd been flying, and Leon had been cheering from the ground. It had felt good, and Hayes had been showing off a bit. He didn't need to with Leon, but he'd been surprised at how good it felt to be flying again. He'd been avoiding it because he felt out of control when he was in the air, and he was, but maybe it wasn't a bad thing.

But it certainly had become bad when he'd lost control.

The wind had picked up, and Hayes had been way too high to control his body. The wind had pushed him away, and no matter how hard Hayes fought against it, he couldn't stop his descent. He'd hoped to crash against a tree or something like that, but instead, he'd slammed into the roof of a home.

Rikar's home.

What were the odds that Hayes would crash into the home

of the guy he'd been thinking about since the night they'd met? Even worse, what were the odds that he'd crash into his mate's home?

Hayes still couldn't make sense of the words. How could he be Rikar's mate? He had no doubt that Rikar was telling the truth, but it still didn't feel right — or rather, it felt *too* right.

Hayes had known in a way, hadn't he? He'd felt drawn to Rikar, and while he'd chalked it up to Rikar being incredibly gorgeous, he'd known there was more to it. He'd never felt this way for anyone, not even the sexiest guy.

He wanted to crawl into Rikar's arms and never leave. He wanted to be there for Rikar, support and protect him, just as much as he wanted to be supported and protected by him. Even though they'd barely met, he could imagine their entire future together.

He groaned and looked up. Apparently, that future was going to start with home renovations.

"I told Leon you were all right," Rikar said as he returned.

"Did you send him home?"

"I explained I'd take care of you, but I wouldn't be surprised if he came back. He was worried."

"That's because we're friends."

Rikar nodded. "Why are you still on the floor?"

Hayes flushed and scrambled to his feet. He didn't want to tell Rikar he was still there because he'd been obsessing over him. He didn't sit on the couch like Rikar had hinted at before, though. Instead, he stared at the mess around him.

He would have to clean this up, at the very least.

He swallowed. He didn't know how to fix this, but he sure as hell was going to try.

"So, I have no idea where to start with your roof, but I'll pay for whatever repairs you need."

"You realize I don't care about the roof, right?"

Hayes shook his head. "How can you not care about the

roof? It's going to rain, and your entire living room will be ruined. We need to do something about it, and fast."

Rikar put his hands on both of Hayes's shoulders, forcing him to stop talking. "Breathe," he ordered.

Hayes nodded and did as Rikar had said. He breathed, trying to push through the panic. Why was he even panicking? Rikar wasn't angry. He wasn't about to beat Hayes up or torture him because he'd broken his roof.

But he was his mate.

Hayes was human. He'd known he could be someone's mate, but he hadn't expected to meet whoever that would be. He and the other mutants were in hiding, and they had far from what he'd call a normal life. He'd always felt it wouldn't be fair to drag a mate into it, but surprise, his mate was already there.

A knock on the door made both of them turn around. Rikar frowned and left Hayes where he was, for which Hayes was grateful. He needed to be alone to even start to understand everything that had just happened.

What the fuck was he supposed to do about the fact that Rikar was his mate?

Rikar hadn't said anything else. He'd just declared that they were mates, and that was that. Hayes wasn't sure if it was because he was still worried or because he was giving Hayes time and space, but he'd need much more than a few minutes.

He could hear voices, but since he had no idea who was at the door, he decided to start cleaning up. It was the least he could do, and before leaving, he'd also make sure the hole was covered. He might not be able to fix it, but he could ensure no water leaked into the house.

Rikar appeared at the living room door again. He looked annoyed, and Hayes quickly understood why when he saw Jessup and Leon behind him. Both of them were flushed and panting, a sure sign that they'd run all the way from the house.

"Your friends are here to check up on you," Rikar said.

Leon glared at him, but Jessup seemed confused by Rikar's reaction to their presence. Explaining to them that Rikar was his mate would make all of this easier to understand, but Hayes had barely wrapped his mind around that fact. He wasn't sure he was ready to tell anyone, not even his best friend.

"What happened to you?" Jessup asked. "Is this what Olga was hinting at?"

She'd been hinting at Hayes and Rikar being mates. She'd known all along, and now that Hayes thought about it, Rikar had known at least since the diner. He was a Nix, which meant he'd have known Hayes was his mate as soon as he saw him.

Yet he hadn't said anything.

Why? Was he hiding something? Had he been planning on never telling Hayes because he didn't want Hayes to be his mate? But that didn't make sense. If he hadn't been planning on telling Hayes, then why had he? Was it just because he'd been afraid for Hayes's safety?

"Hayes?" Jessup asked.

His voice was soft and gentle, as if he were afraid to spook Hayes. That wasn't too far from the truth, but Hayes decided to push all of that away. "We need to clean up," he said.

"If they want to help, they can clean up, but I'm taking you to the bathroom to take care of those scratches," Rikar declared.

His voice had authority, which made sense since he was the tribe leader. Technically, he shouldn't be ordering the mutants around, but he supposed that wasn't exactly what he was doing.

"You should at least wash your face," Leon agreed. "I can

take a better look once you're done."

Rikar glared at him. "I'll take care of him."

"So can I. He's my friend, not yours."

Hayes didn't want his friends and his mate to start bickering over him. "I'll go wash my face," he said before leaving the living room.

The problem was that he had no idea where the bathroom was.

Rikar was behaving like a child, which wasn't like him. It made sense because he wanted to protect Hayes and make sure he was all right, but he wasn't the only one who cared about Hayes. Hayes's friends were here to check on him and make sure he hadn't hurt himself, and there was no reason for Rikar to be jealous.

"I'll show him where the bathroom is," he said.

"We're not here to clean up this mess," Leon called out after Rikar.

Rikar couldn't have cared less if they cleaned his living room. His only focus was Hayes, who was standing in the hallway, looking lost. Rikar took his hand and gently guided him farther into the house, relieved when Hayes didn't protest. Maybe this hadn't been the best moment to tell him they were mates. He'd already been frantic about crashing through the roof, and telling him about their bond hadn't made things easier on him.

"I apologize," Rikar said stiffly.

"What for?"

"For dumping this news on you. I should have known better than to tell you when you were already overwhelmed."

"You mean that you're apologizing for telling me I'm your mate?"

Rikar nodded as he pushed open the bathroom door. He

tugged Hayes inside and toward the closed toilet, then had to let him go to grab his first aid kit. He could easily heal the scratches and cuts on Hayes's hands and face, but first, he'd have to clean them.

"Does anything hurt?" he asked.

Hayes stared at him for a moment before shaking his head. "I'm fine. I managed to slow down my fall, although I'm sorry about what happened. I should have known better."

"What were you doing?" Rikar took out the cotton balls and disinfectant from the box he'd grabbed from under the sink.

"Training."

"On my roof?" Because Rikar couldn't imagine another scenario that would end in Hayes falling through his roof.

"Not exactly." Hayes hesitated. "You know every mutant has a special ability, right? That's why we decided to stick together after we found each other."

"I'm aware of that, although I don't know what your abilities are," Rikar said. He drenched one of the cotton balls in disinfectant, then pressed it on the bigger cut on Hayes's cheek. Hayes winced, but he stayed still and allowed Rikar to clean up the small amount of blood that stained his skin.

"Well, I can fly."

Rikar frowned. "Like a bird?"

Hayes chuckled. "I guess? People usually ask me if I can fly like Superman, though."

"Well? Can you?"

"I don't have to flap my arms like wings. I can just rise into the air and fly around. I have no idea how it works. I just know it does."

"So you were training that ability."

"Yeah. I'll admit I'm not good at it. I don't like feeling out of control, so I tend to avoid flying unless I have to. Olga and Moore pointed out that I need to be ready for the next raid, though, and they're right. I'm here to make a difference, and I won't be able to if I don't know how to use this ability."

Rikar used another cotton ball. "I'm sure you have many more qualities that make you indispensable to your friends."

"Maybe, but this is the only one that's useful to our mission."

"Well, maybe next time you need to find a place with no homes nearby."

Hayes's cheeks flushed. "I will. I'm sorry, and I promise I'll help you fix the roof."

Rikar put everything down and looked at the cuts. Hayes would be fine, and Rikar needed to stop freaking out. He raised his hands and started healing them one by one, the soft light coming from his palms illuminating Hayes's skin.

"I don't expect anything from you," he said. He realized how his words could be taken too late, and he hoped Hayes would understand what he'd been trying to say. He was talking about the roof, not about their relationship.

Hayes hesitated, then nodded. "I'll still help with the roof." He swallowed heavily. "What you said earlier about me being your mate. Is it the truth?" His voice had gone quiet, but Rikar wasn't sure it was because he didn't want his friends to possibly overhear their conversation.

It was almost as if he couldn't quite believe that he was Rikar's mate and that saying the words out loud might ruin his chances to be.

"I wouldn't lie about something like that. Yes, you're my mate."

Hayes nodded. "What about that guy?"

It took Rikar a moment to understand who Hayes was talking about. "Kamrey?"

"I don't know his name, but you were on a date the night we met."

"My mothers organized a blind date. Actually, they didn't

as much as organize it as ambush me with it. They knew I would say no if they asked me outright, so they told me to come to dinner with them, and once I was there, they left and abandoned me with Kamrey. I didn't want to be rude, so I agreed to have dinner with him."

"Why didn't you want to go on a date? He was cute."

"I wasn't looking for a relationship."

Hayes slowly nodded. "And now, you've changed your mind?"

Rikar sighed and leaned back against the sink. "I'll be honest with you. I don't know what I want. I have good reasons not to wish for a relationship right now, and I'm sure you can understand them. The tribe and the town are growing, and it's becoming harder and harder to be a leader for both. It takes most of my time and my energy, and I don't feel I can be a good mate in this situation."

"So you're rejecting me?" Hayes's voice trembled, and Rikar hated himself for hurting him.

"I'm messing this up," he said as he raked a hand through his hair. "I'm not rejecting you. I'm just trying to wrap my mind around what's happening. If you were anyone else, I would tell you that I don't want a relationship. But you're my mate. I can't give up this relationship without at least trying. I'd never forgive myself if I did, plus I don't want to hurt you. But I realize both our lives are complicated."

"It sounds like you're trying to convince yourself that it would be better if we stayed away from each other," Hayes murmured.

Was he hearing the words Rikar was saying? Or was Rikar maybe saying the wrong ones?

He stepped forward and took Hayes's hands in his. "I'm not trying to convince myself of anything. I'm also not rejecting you. I'm trying to say that while I know both our lives are complicated and full already, I'm not giving up on you. I don't know what our relationship will be like, but I want to find out."

Hayes stared at their linked hands.

Rikar wished he could feel Hayes's emotions already, but they weren't bonded. The only way for him to understand what was going on in Hayes's mind was to wait for Hayes to explain.

"You didn't tell me I was your mate when you first realized it," Hayes said.

Hayes was hurt by that. Rikar could see it. "To be honest, I was in shock. The last thing I expected while I was on a blind date my mother organized was to look up and see the most beautiful man in the world and realize he was my mate. I wanted to tell you right then, but I didn't want to make things awkward and uncomfortable. You weren't alone, and Kamrey was there, and we were in the middle of the diner."

"I guess I can understand that. But you still didn't come to me later. Would you have talked to me at all if I hadn't crashed through your roof?"

"I would have. I was trying to find the perfect moment, which in hindsight, was ridiculous. You didn't need a perfect moment for me to tell you you're my mate. You just needed me to be honest." And Rikar hadn't been, but he swore to himself from now on, he would be. It was the least he could do for himself and for Hayes.

He didn't know where this conversation left them, but he didn't need to. He'd give Hayes time to wrap his mind around their bond and what it meant for both of them, and hopefully, by the time he had, he'd be ready to talk again.

CHAPTER THREE

Moore looked around their group. "Ready?"

Everyone nodded, although Hayes wondered if they were as ready as they acted. He certainly wasn't. But then he never felt ready, so maybe he was. There was only one way for him to know, and it was to throw himself into the action.

The team that would be going on the raid had met at the house Moore shared with his mate. Not all mutants participated in all the raids because it would be too many people trying to fit into a limited space and be inconspicuous. Discretion was a must in this job, so it was better to go in small groups. Usually there weren't more than ten participants, maybe a dozen. As long as the lab they were raiding wasn't too large, they could neutralize the guards and scientists, explore its entirety, and rescue everyone they found that needed rescuing.

Hayes's job was recon. Before heading out, they gathered all the information they could find because it would be too dangerous not to, but Hayes always got in the air and looked around before giving Moore the go-ahead. He also kept an eye on the area while the raid was happening, so he seldom had anything to do with fighting. That was good because he wouldn't have known where to start.

Moore left his living room, and everyone filed behind him. Jolyn stayed back, a small frown on his face. He still wasn't used to watching his mate leave to go raid labs, although Hayes supposed he had some experience when it came to that. He worked for the council assassins, which meant watching them go on missions, and sometimes, watching them come back wounded. Hayes had no doubt that was what was going through Jolyn's mind right now. He didn't want his mate to get hurt, and he was worried that was what would happen.

Hayes's thoughts moved to his own mate. He had no idea where he and Rikar stood. After the disaster of Hayes crashing through Rikar's roof, Hayes had been avoiding the man. He knew they needed to talk, and soon, but what was he supposed to do? He understood why Rikar hadn't told him right away they were mates, and even why Rikar had waited days after he realized it. It was a lot to wrap your mind around, and Hayes himself had trouble doing so. At the same time, though, he felt hurt. Meeting your mate was a joyful thing in a shifter's life, as it was for a Nix. Rikar should have been happy, but instead, it looked like he was trying to convince Hayes that it would be better for them to be apart. Hayes wasn't sure he agreed. The problem was that he also wasn't sure he disagreed.

He climbed down the porch steps, ready to follow the others, but he blinked when he saw Rikar standing there. He looked around, thinking that maybe Rikar was here for someone else. That couldn't be right, though, and deep inside, he was very much aware of that.

"What are you doing here?" he asked when he reached his mate.

Rikar's smile was tense. "I just wanted to see you."

Hayes frowned and crossed his arms over his chest. Was Rikar going to ask him to stay behind? Even if Rikar wasn't sure he wanted Hayes in his life, Hayes was still his mate. If something happened to him, Rikar would be hurt, no matter their relationship. It was tempting to stay back, if anything because Hayes wasn't a hero. He didn't want to get hurt or risk his life, but he doubted anyone was happy to do so.

But they did it anyway because they felt it was their duty.

Hayes certainly did. He'd been rescued from the lab he'd been kept in, and he wouldn't have been if someone hadn't gone out there and put themselves in danger for him. The least he could do now was do the same for other people in the same position he'd been in recently.

But Rikar didn't ask Hayes to stay back. Instead, he stared at him until Hayes wanted to shuffle his feet. He was already nervous because of the raid. Did Rikar have to make things worse?

"What do you want?" Hayes asked.

"To tell you to be careful."

Hayes blinked. "I always am. Why would you need to come here to tell me that?"

The corner of Rikar's lips curled. "Why wouldn't I? You're my mate, even though we're not bonded yet." He grimaced. "And let me tell you, that's something I'm tempted to rectify right now."

Hayes's eyes widened. "What are you talking about?"

Rikar rubbed his face with both his hands. "Nothing, just that I'm terrified something's going to happen to you before we have time to sit and talk about our relationship."

"We don't have a relationship." Not right now, anyway. Maybe in the future? Rikar was certainly giving Hayes hope by being here and being worried about him.

"And that's why we need to talk. But even though we're not together, we're still mates, and you still matter to me. I'll be waiting for you when you come home."

"I'll come and see you if it's that important for you."

"It is, please. I need to know you're all right because otherwise I'll freak out, and no one wants that."

"Then I'll come. But don't worry if it takes us a while. I don't know what we'll find there exactly." Thanks to the hackers in their group, they always had an idea, but it didn't mean the information they got was always correct. More than once, they'd had surprises, and not good ones.

Rikar looked around. He and Hayes weren't the only ones saying their goodbyes since Jolyn had followed Moore outside, and the fact that everyone else was focused on other people meant they were in a small bubble of privacy. Whatever he was looking for, Rikar seemed to make a decision. He nodded quickly, then stepped closer to Hayes. Hayes held his breath, waiting to see what his mate would do.

It was nothing he'd expected.

Rikar cupped a hand around Hayes's cheek and pulled him closer. Hayes yielded willingly, excitedly, because he couldn't wait to find out how kissing Rikar felt. He didn't have to wait long because soft flips landed on his.

He breathed out. His shoulders relaxed as if of their own volition, and he leaned against Rikar. The kiss only lasted a few seconds, but it was enough.

Hayes was wanted.

He hadn't known what to think of Rikar's behavior, and he had no idea where they stood, but one thing he was sure of.

Rikar wanted him in his life.

They'd have to talk and work things out, but as long as Hayes knew there was a place for him in Rikar's life, he could allow himself to relax. It would help him focus on the mission, and he had even more incentives to come back now.

He needed to come back if he wanted to find out what would happen between him and his mate.

"It's time to go!" Moore declared.

Hayes glared at him because he wanted more time with Rikar, but he could get that later. For now, he and his team had work to do, and that was what he had to focus on.

"I'll see you soon," Rikar promised.

"You will. Don't worry too much about me. I don't usually fight."

"It's that *usually* that worries me," Rikar said with a smile.

Hayes stepped away from him and closer to Elsa. She and Teddy were Nix, which meant they would shimmer all of them to their destination. It also meant that they were in charge of making sure everyone made it home as well as using their abilities when needed. Teddy's especially came in handy during missions since he could make things explode with just a blink of his eyes. As for Elsa, her power was manipulation of electromagnetic fields, which also was a good addition on missions—although Hayes couldn't have explained why because he and Physics had never been friends.

Sometimes Hayes felt like the odd man out. He reminded himself that he was still doing something good. He made sure everything looked safe and that when his friends and family went in, they had a better idea of what they'd encounter.

Elsa winked at him, and the town around them vanished in the blink of an eye.

Time to get to work.

Rikar watched the mutants vanish. His focus stayed on the spot where Hayes had been standing only seconds before, and worry gnawed at his gut.

Would Hayes be okay? What if something happened to him?

Rikar was tempted to follow Hayes to the lab, but he stayed where he was. It wasn't the first time Hayes went on a mission, and it wouldn't be the last. This was important to Hayes, just like it was to the other mutants, and Rikar needed to respect that. Hayes wouldn't be doing it if he didn't feel like he had to, and it wasn't Rikar's place to tell him to stop.

Besides, he didn't *want* Hayes to stop. He and others in the village had been raiding labs since they were created, long before shifters and other paranormal creatures became common knowledge amongst humans. They'd saved hundreds of people, and to do so, they'd had to raid labs. If anything, the mutants were better equipped than Rikar had ever been. They had powers Rikar couldn't even begin to imagine, and they knew how to use them.

Well, Hayes wasn't great at his, but hopefully, he wouldn't crash through anyone's roof today.

Rikar would never ask Hayes to stop doing this. He'd never know what it was like to be in a lab, experimented on, and changed. He'd never know what it was like to go through that pain and horror, to lose everything twice. But he'd seen enough to know that if Hayes was doing this, it was necessary to his well-being. It was probably his way of dealing with the memories and the pain, and that was fine.

Since there was nothing he could do, he gave Jolyn a tight smile and headed toward his house. He didn't think he could stay with people at the moment. He'd be too annoying, and no one wanted that. No, Rikar needed space, and his home was the best place to get that. That way, if people needed him, they'd be able to find him, but if no one did, he'd be left alone.

He left his shoes by the front door and walked into the living room barefoot. The plastic tarps he'd used to cover the hole in his roof rustled with the wind, making him look up.

That was something else he needed to take care of. With the weather turning colder, he couldn't afford to have this hole in his roof for much longer. It would become a problem once it started raining more, and the cold was already getting to him. Hayes had promised he'd fix it, but Rikar didn't need him to. He just needed *someone* to fix it. It didn't have to be Hayes.

Rikar made a few phone calls as he paced the length of his living room. Being a tribe leader and unofficial mayor of a small town came with a lot of responsibilities and work, but it also had its perks. Almost everyone he called had an opening to come and see the hole in his roof, so he had his choice of companies. He picked the one who seemed more reasonably priced, feeling relieved once the phone call was over and knowing he'd have a new roof in just a few days.

When his phone rang, he prayed it wasn't the company changing their mind. When he saw Moore's name flashing on the screen, the bottom of his stomach felt like it'd dropped out.

Rikar's fingers trembled as he answered the call. "Moore?"

"Everyone is fine," Moore declared. "Including Hayes."

Rikar blinked, because that wasn't what he'd expected. He was glad Moore had thought of informing him of that right away, though. "Thank you for telling me that."

"I knew you'd be worried. But we have a situation."

The bad feeling came back. It could be anything, from the lab being too secure for them to go in to something they'd found inside. Rikar had stumbled onto nasty situations a few times himself, so he knew what to expect and that sometimes, unexpected things happened. "What is it?"

"I need you to come here."

"So something did happen?"

"We have a few scratches and whatnot, but I swear everyone is fine. The team isn't the problem. Look, I think it would be easier for you to understand if you came here."

"I'll be there in seconds. Who should I focus on?"

"We took down the shields, so you can focus on me. I'll see you soon."

Moore hung up, and Rikar did the same on his end. He rushed to his front door, pushed his feet into his shoes, and shimmered immediately, using Moore as an anchor.

The man was standing by an open door when Rikar reached him, and Rikar took a few seconds to look Moore up and down and reassure himself that he truly was okay. He and Moore weren't friends, but they were friendly, and Rikar didn't want anyone to get hurt.

"I'm sorry I had to call you," Moore said.

"I told you that you could call anytime you needed something, and I wasn't lying."

Moore nodded. He had his arms crossed over his chest and a worried expression on his face. "That's good, because we need your help."

Rikar stared at him for a second. He was trying to read Moore's expression, but it was almost impossible. There was worry there, but it wasn't the only emotion. "Whatever I can do, I'll do," Rikar promised.

Moore shook his head. "I wouldn't make that kind of promise until you've seen what we found."

"Show me."

Moore nodded and uncrossed his arms, then took a step forward. He headed toward the open door, and Rikar followed him. "Through the files we were able to hack, we knew that this lab had between fifteen and twenty patients, as they call them. We weren't able to find out how many exactly because they tend to move people around, and some of them die." Moore's expression hardened. "So we kept twenty in mind as we came in. The guards and the scientists weren't a problem. To be honest, they were kind of sloppy, but this is a private lab. I'd expect something different from the government, but the private labs are always easier to get into."

"I'm aware of that. Why don't you just tell me what happened?"

"I'm getting there." Moore sucked in a breath as he stopped moving. "It's children, Rikar."

It took Rikar a few seconds to understand what Moore was saying. "You mean those twenty patients are children?"

Moore's expression was grim. "We didn't expect that. All the patients we found in the files had numbers. There are no names, and only a few had birthdates, but we kind of skipped over those. We've never found children." His hand trembled as he reached up to rake a hand through his hair. "I never expected anyone to do something like this. It's too horrible. I mean, torturing adults is one thing, but kids?"

Rikar was as horrified as Moore, and he hadn't even seen the kids yet. He needed to keep his calm, especially if Moore was going to break down. The man was visibly doing his best to keep calm, but it wasn't working.

Rikar didn't blame him. Experimenting on anyone was horrifying, but doing it to children was the true sign of a monster.

"So you're going to see two rows of cages when you go into that room," Moore said. "I'm telling you this so you're ready, because we weren't. What's in that room is, well, I don't even have words. I've never seen anything like that, and I hope I never see anything like that again. I'm going to have nightmares."

Rikar squeezed one of Moore's shoulders. He had no doubt he'd have nightmares, too, but that wouldn't stop either of them from going into that room. Those children were innocent. What had been done to them was awful, and while they couldn't do anything to fix the past, they could do everything in their power to make the future as painless as possible for those children. If they had even only one opportunity to survive this, Rikar and Moore would give it to them.

Hayes couldn't look away. He knew he should because what was in front of him was horrifying, but he felt some kind of kinship with these children. He'd been where they were. He'd been in a cage, in pain, lost, and wondering what was happening to his body.

But at least he'd been an adult. He'd known what they were doing to him, that the torturers had a reason. He'd known they didn't care about him and that they would ignore his cries for help and his tears.

But these kids were just that. They were *children*, and even the oldest kids Hayes could see he couldn't fully understand what was happening to them. It made Hayes want to find the scientists they'd locked up in the closet and kill them with his bare hands. He didn't care that he didn't know how to fight, that he was human and couldn't inflict much pain. He wanted to kick, scream, and demand to know why they'd done this.

He swallowed. He wasn't alone in the room, and he was glad to have Jessup by his side. Jessup's ability was mind control, and right now, he was using it on the children. He kept them calm until Moore decided what to do and got help.

The strain showed. Jessup had said that it would be easier to control these kids because some of them were unconscious or asleep, and the others were in bad shape, but he still had to divide up his focus on almost twenty kids. He wouldn't be able to keep it up much longer, and Hayes wished Moore would hurry up. He'd stepped outside, telling them he was getting help, but he hadn't been back yet.

The sound of footsteps made Hayes turn. He was relieved to see Moore and surprised to see Rikar behind him. "When you said you were getting help, I thought you were calling the assassins," he said.

"They're next on my list. I just wanted someone on our side."

Hayes didn't roll his eyes, considering the dire situation, but it was tempting. "The assassins are on our side, too. Just because they work for the council doesn't mean they're enemies. You should know that, considering your mate works for them."

"I called Rikar because I want these kids to have a choice. We both know that once the council finds out about this, they'll put the kids in the hospital, and then they'll vanish. I don't trust the council to take the children back to their parents."

Hayes disagreed, but now wasn't the moment to say it. Besides, he was glad to see Rikar, too. His presence made Hayes feel more capable of dealing with the horror in front of him.

Rikar's eyes were wide as he looked down the two rows of cages. There was a row on each side of the room, leaving enough space between them that people could walk down the path. All the cages were locked, but Moore had already *convinced* one of the scientists to give him the code. Now, they just needed to get the kids out.

Hayes didn't know how they were going to do it.

"You still need to call the assassins," Rikar said. "I'd offer homes to all of these children, but they're going to need help, and that's way beyond what I can do for them. I have no problem taking the children who are the healthiest back to the village, but our clinic can't handle so many ill kids."

But they weren't ill. They'd been tortured, and there was no way to know what had been done to them until they went over the files. Moore had to see that the assassins and the council would be better equipped to deal with all of this.

Hayes hoped he did.

He stepped toward the closest cage. A little girl was curled up in a fetal position at the back. Her feet were bare, her dark hair covered her face, and she was only wearing a hospital gown. Even with that on, Hayes could see bulky bandages wrapped around her torso. She was breathing, but there was no way to know if she was in shock or still under Jessup's control.

"Jessup, I need you to let go," Moore said.

"You're sure?" Jessup asked, even though he was pale and sweaty.

"Yes. I need to explain what's going on to these children, and we have to talk to every single one of them. I also don't want you to control them more than necessary. They need to feel in control after what was done to them."

Hayes couldn't say he disagreed, but it wouldn't be easy. It never was, and they were talking about children this time around.

Jessup nodded curtly, and as soon as his shoulders sagged, someone in the room started screaming.

It wasn't the little girl Hayes was standing next to. It was someone down the row of cages, but Hayes couldn't see who.

The other mutants came into the room, and they went to work without talking to each other. Hayes left the first girl to Jessup since she seemed to be in shock and moved on to the cage next to hers.

Inside was a tiny cheetah shifter. Hayes couldn't tell if they were a girl or boy, but it didn't matter.

"Hi there," Rikar said as he moved behind Hayes. He curled his fingers around one of the bars of the cages while reaching for the touchpad that kept it locked with the other. He quickly typed, but he didn't open the cage right away.

"My name is Rikar, and as you can see, I'm a Nix. Me and everyone else here want to help you, but we can only do that if you don't attack us."

Being attacked by a cheetah, even one so small, could kill someone, especially a human like Hayes. He took a step back, more than happy to let Rikar take control of the situation.

The cage door squeaked when it opened. The cheetah stayed where they were at the back of the cage for a moment, but as soon as Rikar was crouched in front of the cage, they threw themselves at him. Hayes cried out, convinced the cheetah was about to eat Rikar's face, but instead, the cheetah turned into a little girl.

Her brown hair was long and wild around her face, and her green eyes were the biggest Hayes had ever seen. They were dark with fear, but she didn't hesitate to wrap herself around Rikar and cling for dear life. She was naked instead of wearing a hospital gown like most of the other children, but she didn't seem to notice. Her eyes were full of tears, and as soon as Rikar wrapped his arms around her, she started crying.

Rikar got to his feet, still holding her. He gently stroked her back, shushing her and speaking so softly that Hayes couldn't hear what he was saying.

Hayes looked around. He wanted to cover the girl, so he snatched one of the white doctor coats that hung on the wall. He quickly went back to Rikar and wrapped the coat around the girl's shoulders. She stiffened but stayed where she was, clearly feeling safe in Rikar's arms.

Hayes wanted to cry. It was incredible that after what had been done to her, she still had enough trust in her tiny body to cling to Rikar the way she was. She was one of the few, too. As Hayes looked around the room, he saw terrified children curled up in their cages, and those were the conscious ones. Several of them hadn't reacted when the mutants had opened their cages, and they worried Hayes more than anyone else.

His gaze caught with Moore's, who was holding a little boy.

"You need to call the assassins," Hayes said.

Moore nodded. "I will. We can't handle this on our own, and I'm very much aware of that."

For the first time since Hayes had met him, he looked as lost as everyone else. That said something about the situation, but Hayes already knew. They were all horrified by what they'd found, and they had no idea how to deal with it.

The little girl clung to Rikar, and he had no idea what to do with her. He wanted to help the other children, even though he could see they were in good hands. The mutants had stepped in, opened all the cages, and they were trying to coax out the children who could be convinced of doing so. Other children were unconscious, and they needed to get medical help as soon as possible.

Thankfully, Moore realized that he and Rikar couldn't deal with this alone. He was still holding the little boy he'd taken out of one of the cages, but with his other hand, he'd taken out his phone.

Rikar looked at the girl in his arms. "I told you my name, but I don't know yours," he murmured.

He smoothed a hand over her dark hair. Her face was tucked against his neck, and she was sniffling, but he couldn't feel the wetness of tears anymore.

"Samara," a whisper answered.

Rikar's heart skipped a beat. "That's a beautiful name. Do you want to meet my mate? His name is Hayes, and he can fly."

Samara finally leaned back to look at a Rikar. There was dirt on her cheek, and she was too thin, but otherwise, she seemed healthy. There was no way for Rikar to know if that was true. Considering what the people in these labs did, there was a good chance Samara had been hurt in ways Rikar couldn't even imagine.

"Like a bird?" she asked.

Rikar smiled. "Not exactly. Do you want to know how we met?"

She pushed away a strand of hair from her face and nodded. Rikar liked that she was interacting with him. She might be in shock, but it wasn't as bad off as some of the other children he could see.

"Well, he crashed through my roof. He was training, but the wind was too strong, and he ended up making a big hole in my roof."

Samara stared at him for a second before asking, "Is the

hole still there?"

"It is. Unfortunately, I haven't yet found the time to fix it."

She stuck her thumb in her mouth and continued staring. She had to be around nine or ten, possibly older, but it was hard to tell. She was too old to suck her thumb, but Rikar wasn't about to scold her for it. She was self-soothing, which at the moment was all that mattered.

"They're coming," Moore declared.

Rikar relaxed. The assassins and the council would know what to do about these kids. He smiled at Samara and looked around for Hayes, who'd reached into one of the cages and was gently moving the unconscious wolf curled at the back of the cage toward the front. He was moving extremely slowly, no doubt so he wouldn't hurt the kid. Rikar held his breath when he saw Hayes press two fingers to the wolf's throat, wondering if it was already too late for the child. When Hayes's shoulders relaxed and he briefly smiled, Rikar knew he was in time.

But it might be if they didn't take the children to the hospital quickly.

Someone suddenly appeared next to Moore. The boy in Moore's arm screamed, and Moore quickly went to work trying to calm him down. Rikar recognized Julian, one of the assassins, and his mate, Tali. There were others with them, and they moved as one, getting to work.

There was little Rikar could do with Samara clinging to him, so he tried to stay out of the way as much as he could and pressed his back against the wall. He watched as a man wearing a white coat that he quickly ditched arrived. He was holding a bag, and there was no doubt in Rikar's mind that this was the assassins' doctor. He wasn't alone, although the second doctor appeared lost. His expression hardened when he saw what was happening around them, and he quickly started working, too.

Everyone was doing everything they could to take care of the children.

"We need to take the unconscious children to a hospital," the assassins' doctor said.

"What about the other ones?" the other doctor asked.

"I think we can take a risk and take them to the infirmary."

Hayes came to stand next to Rikar, so Rikar asked, "Can you tell me who these people are?"

Hayes nodded and started pointing. "The one in charge is Rocco. He was an assassin, but now he's the assassins' doctor. The guy with him is with the assassins to help one of the guys they rescued from a lab. Jasper found his mate in the assassins and has been staying with them."

"So they have some knowledge when it comes to these situations?"

"Yeah. I don't know if Rocco has ever worked with kids, but the assassins have. They saved a bunch of them several years ago."

Rikar smiled. "How do you know so much about them?"

"Well, Jolyn has been telling us a lot of stuff. He wants Moore to see the assassins as friends rather than people he can't trust. I guess he's trying to make them look more human. In the end, they're like us. The only difference is that they work for the council."

They appeared very much human to Rikar. He saw tears in the eyes of several of them, while others had a fierce expression that said that if they got their hands on the scientists who'd been hurting these children, they wouldn't hesitate to kill them. Rikar couldn't say he disagreed. He wanted to do the same.

The Nix started shimmering the unconscious children away. Some of the conscious children went along since Rocco had declared their wounds were too important to treat in the infirmary. Rikar wasn't sure what infirmary he was talking about, but he supposed he was about to find out. If Samara didn't let go of him, he'd have to go with her.

"What about the other kids?" Moore asked. The little boy he'd been carrying was still in his arms.

"We'll take them to our infirmary," Rocco said. He hesitated. "If you want, some of you can come with us. They're waiting for us, and it's obvious some of the kids have latched onto you. I don't want to separate them from the one person they feel safe with."

"Besides, it's not as if I've never seen where you live," Moore said, a tiny smile curling the corner of his lips.

In the end, Moore, Rikar, Hayes, Leon, and Jasmine went along for the ride. Each of them carried a child while the other Nix took care of the others. Rikar allowed Jolyn to shimmer him wherever they were going since he had no idea where that was. As soon as they arrived, Jolyn disappeared, no doubt going back to get more of the children.

Rikar looked around. They were in a wide, clean infirmary. Several people hovered by the door, but they rushed forward as soon as the children arrived. Some children started crying, others screamed, and while Rikar wanted to help all of them, he focused on Samara.

"How do you feel about doctors?" he asked her.

She shuddered. "They're bad." Rikar wasn't surprised that was her opinion. "Well, I think that some doctors are bad, but others are good."

"He's right," Hayes said. "Do you know why I can fly?"

Samara peered at him, shaking her head. Her hair brushed against Rikar's jaw, and he smoothed it down. It was a tangled mess.

Hayes's smile was easy, but Rikar could see the pain in his eyes. "Well, once, I was in a cage like you. Some doctors hurt me, and I hated them. They're the reason I can fly, and while I don't like doctors, Rocco and his friends only want to help.

They want to make sure you're all right."

Samara was still hesitant, but she agreed to let Rikar place her on one of the beds.

It took hours to check all the children. After Rocco had, he admitted it would take even longer to find out what had been done to them and what it meant for their future. But once he was done checking all of them, it was time to find them a safe place to live until their parents or an adult responsible for them could be located. They couldn't stay in the infirmary or in the warehouse with the assassins.

"I can take them to my tribe," Rikar offered for the second time tonight. Samara was in his arms again, fast asleep this time. He was sitting at Rocco's desk, with Rocco slumped into a chair, Hayes and Rob, the other doctor, sitting on the closest bed, and Win, the assassins' handler, standing by them.

Win appeared relieved. "I know it's a lot to ask, but we can't keep them here," he said.

"I'm aware of that, and I don't have a problem taking them in." It would take some rearranging, but everyone in the tribe would be happy to welcome these children. Many tribe members would understand what the children had been through because they'd been in those labs, too. Hopefully, that would help.

That didn't mean the next steps would be easy. If anything, they would no doubt be challenging, but these children deserved a future. They'd almost lost everything, and Rikar wanted to give them back all of it.

CHAPTER FOUR

It was time to help with the roof.

Hayes was still bewildered by what he'd seen yesterday at the lab. It had taken them hours to take care of all the children, and by the time every single one of them had a bed for the foreseeable future and a safe place to rest and heal, Hayes and the others had been exhausted. Rikar had taken Samara home, while Hayes had slumped in his bed and fallen asleep. He'd slept for twelve hours, but now he was awake and needed to do something.

He still didn't understand where he and Rikar stood. He wanted them to talk about it, but he had no idea where to start or if it would be wise. Maybe it would be better for him not to find out what Rikar wanted. The thought that Rikar might reject him was terrifying and almost enough to keep him where he was.

But Hayes couldn't continue wondering and hoping but never knowing. As tempting as it was, hiding his head in the sand wouldn't solve anything. If Rikar felt they shouldn't be together, then Hayes needed to know. That way he could take the next step and make decisions about his life.

He hauled himself out of bed and headed to the bathroom. His phone vibrated on his nightstand, but since he saw it was his mother, he didn't bother answering. He'd texted her that he'd let her know when he could come, but that wasn't enough for her. She wanted a date, and soon.

Hayes hadn't told her that he'd rescued a bunch of children from being tortured yesterday. She didn't need to know what was happening in the world. She didn't need to know what state the children had been in, and that at least a few of them were still at the hospital, unconscious. Hayes wanted his mother to understand where he was coming from but not to be aware of what still happened in the labs. No one needed to be burdened with that, especially people who couldn't do anything to help.

But Hayes *could* do something to help. He had, and it made him feel better about going to dinner and telling his mother that he wasn't moving back home.

That didn't mean he was looking forward to doing so.

He'd showered yesterday, so he quickly used the toilet, washed his face and hands, and went back to the bedroom. Since his mother had hung up, he texted her so she wouldn't continue calling, dressed, and headed downstairs.

Elsa and Jessup were already in the kitchen. Elsa was staring at a steaming mug of coffee while Jessup poked at a bowl of cereal. Neither of them looked very awake, and Hayes could see signs that they were still thinking about yesterday like he was. The things they'd found in that lab weren't something they could forget anytime soon, and Hayes suspected they'd have nightmares for weeks to come. He'd woken up from one around two AM, and he hadn't been able to go back to sleep until much later.

The three of them were silent as Hayes got himself a cup of coffee. He wasn't hungry, and he felt like he'd never be hungry again.

"Where are you going?" Jessup finally asked as Hayes was leaving the kitchen.

"To Rikar's. I still need to help him with the roof."

"I should come, too," he said.

"Why? I'm the one who fell through the roof, not you."

The corner of Jessup's lips curled in a smile. "I wish I'd been there to see it."

"Leon would tell you it was better you weren't because it was terrifying." It had been. Hayes had been convinced he'd hurt himself and was extremely lucky he hadn't. The only wounds he'd sported after that had been cuts and scratches, which Rikar had healed. It could have been much worse.

"I saw the two of you yesterday," Jessup said.

Hayes had told him Rikar was his mate as soon as they'd come home after the botched training. Jessup and Leon had dragged Hayes home to make sure he was all right, which he was. He'd needed to tell his best friend about the bond, and since then, Jessup had been gently asking what Hayes would do about Rikar.

"What did you see?"

Elsa snorted. "Everyone saw the two of you kiss," she pointed out. "We've been talking about it, and by *we*, I mean all of us."

Right. When Rikar had come to see Hayes off before the raid, he'd kissed him.

"Why's everyone talking about it?" he asked, already knowing the answer. They were his family, that was why.

"We're curious, but since you haven't told us anything, we figure you need time."

Hayes was grateful. "I do." He looked at Jessup. "But I promise we'll talk tonight."

Jessup stared for a moment before nodding. "As long as he's not hurting you."

"He's not." At least, not for now. It might be different if Rikar decided he didn't want Hayes, but that wasn't so. He did want him. It was just complicated for both of them to make a place in their life for the other.

Reminding himself of that made Hayes feel lighter as he walked toward Rikar's home. It was still early in the morning, but he couldn't sleep any more, so he was glad he was already out of the house. The days after raids were always harsh, but this time especially. Yesterday had been a reminder of what all of them had gone through. It had shown them how cruel some humans could be in vivid detail. They'd already known that some people were monsters, but Hayes hadn't believed it could get that bad.

He should have known better.

Only one light was on in Rikar's house when Hayes reached it. He knocked on the door and waited, smiling when he heard Rikar reach the door. When he opened it, he was wearing a pair of pants that looked soft, a big t-shirt, and nothing else. His feet were bare, and his long blond hair clearly hadn't been combed yet.

Hayes's fingers itched with the need to do it himself.

"Had we agreed to meet this morning?" he asked softly, looking behind himself.

"No, but I decided that today was the best day for me to fix your roof."

Rikar frowned. "I already told you that you don't have to do it. I called several companies, and someone's coming today."

That would probably be for the best, since Hayes had no idea where to start fixing a roof. "The least I can do is go up there and make sure it's well covered for the moment."

"You can certainly do that, but it's not necessary."

"Please. It would help me feel less guilty."

Rikar finally smiled. "All right, but only if I come with you."

Hayes found himself grinning. "Are you afraid I'll fall through the roof again if you don't?"

"A bit." He looked down at himself. "Let me put my shoes on."

Hayes tried to peek around him, but he couldn't see anyone else in the home. "Where's Samara?"

"Still asleep. She had several nightmares during the night."

That would explain why Rikar looked exhausted. It didn't surprise Hayes after the nightmare he'd had. Seeing the kids in those cages had brought back memories he'd rather never think about again, and it was always hard to deal with. He could only imagine what Samara was dealing with.

It took only a few seconds for Rikar to be ready. When he was, he stepped on the porch and closed the door behind himself. Then he looked at Hayes. "How are we getting up there? Want me to shimmer you?"

Hayes shook his head, making a decision he hoped he wouldn't regret. "Let me fly you up."

Rikar's eyes widened, but he nodded. "I trust you."

"At least if we crash through a roof, it'll be *your* roof."

Rikar laughed and stepped into Hayes's arms. It wasn't the first time Hayes had taken someone with him when he flew, but Rikar was the most precious person he'd ever taken up. He was careful as he pushed off the ground and into the air, and it was worth seeing the smile bloom on Rikar's lips.

The flight was short, and only a few seconds later, they landed on the roof. Hayes kept a hold on Rikar to make sure he was steady on his feet, then let go once he was.

But Rikar didn't go anywhere. He stayed put, close enough to kiss Hayes.

And he did.

Hayes sighed in pleasure and closed his eyes. He wrapped his arms around Rikar's neck and allowed his mate to pull him closer. He felt safe here, even though they were on a roof next to a hole he'd made. Rikar wouldn't let him fall, and if he did, he'd shimmer Hayes to safety.

Maybe that was what Hayes needed to feel more secure of his ability and life in general. He needed to know someone would catch him if he fell, and now, he did.

The kiss was marvelous, and Rikar was glad he'd taken this risk. He wasn't sure where he and Hayes stood when it came to their relationship, and they needed to talk about it, but that could wait, at least for a few moments. Hayes felt perfect in Rikar's arms, and Rikar never wanted to let go.

Hopefully, he wouldn't have to.

But both their lives had gotten even more complicated with Samara's presence, and that was something else they'd need to talk about. Samara had told Hayes that she didn't have parents anymore. She'd been in the human foster system before she was taken, which meant she didn't have a family to go back to. Rikar wouldn't allow anyone to put her back in that system when she needed a home, a family, and someone who would make sure she healed from what she'd gone through, both physically and mentally.

He didn't know if that someone would be him, but he would if no one else volunteered. He just hoped it wouldn't cost him his mate.

"Rikar!" someone screamed from inside the house.

Rikar jerked away from Hayes, almost stumbling. Hayes caught him before he could step into the hole behind him and crash down in his living room.

"It's Samara," Rikar said. She sounded terrified, which wasn't surprising if she'd woken up to find him gone.

Hayes nodded. "Shimmer us in the house."

Hayes was still holding Rikar's arm, so it only took a few seconds for them to appear in the kitchen, where Samara was. She was in the middle of the room, wearing one of Rikar's old t-shirts that fell to her knees, looking terrified. As soon as he appeared, she threw himself into his arms, and he had to step away from Hayes to grab her.

"I thought you left me," she said.

He stroked her wild hair. "Never."

"You weren't there, like my mom. She was gone when I

woke up, too."

Rikar told himself that he didn't know the entire story behind what Samara had just said and that it wouldn't be the best idea for him to try to find and hunt down her mother.

"We were looking at the hole I made in the roof," Hayes said. "Did you see it yesterday?"

Samara leaned away from Rikar, but she didn't let go of him. "It's big," she said.

Hayes smiled easily. "It really is, and we need to fix it before it rains. That's why we were on the roof."

She nodded, still clinging to Rikar. Rikar doubted she'd let him go easily, but he had to take care of her.

He'd convinced her to shower yesterday and had to help her with her hair. He suspected they'd have to cut part of it because it was too tangled. They'd need a bunch of things, from new clothes to everything else a little girl would need. Rikar wasn't thinking about school yet, especially since he didn't know if Samara had any family other than the mother who'd abandoned her. He was trying not to get attached, but it was hard when she hugged him like this and looked at him as if she knew he'd protect her against everything and anything.

Physically, Samara was fine. Rocco had found scars on her body, and she had a still-healing wound on her thigh, but it didn't look like it bothered her. It was too soon to know what the scientists and doctors had done to her in that lab. Rocco had promised that as soon as he went over the documents the mutants and assassins had found in the lab, he'd let Rikar know. In the meantime, Rikar would treat Samara as he would any other child.

"How about breakfast?" Hayes offered.

That made Samara finally step away from Rikar. "Pancakes?" she asked hopefully.

Hayes grinned. "Pancakes it is, as long as Rikar has all the ingredients."

Samara nodded. "He does. I saw them in the fridge."

Rikar blinked because he hadn't expected that, just like he didn't expect it when Samara moved away from him to take one of Hayes's hands. She pulled him toward the fridge, and Hayes went easily, still staring at Rikar.

Rikar's phone chose that moment to ring. He kept an eye on Samara and Hayes, but they seemed to be okay with each other. She'd been terrified of everyone else yesterday, but Hayes had stuck with them through all of it. She clearly remembered him and somewhat trusted him, which was a relief.

Rikar answered his phone, stepping toward the kitchen door but not leaving the room entirely. "Yes?"

"I'm not surprised to find you already awake," Win said.

It wasn't the first time the tribe and the assassins worked together, and Rikar and Win had a good relationship. That was one of the reasons Rikar hadn't hesitated to offer to take several of the children back to the tribe. It was also why Win had so readily agreed. He'd known they would be safe.

"Sleep wasn't easy," Rikar confirmed.

"I didn't see those kids in the cages, but it wasn't easy for me, either. How's Samara?"

Rikar looked at her. She and Hayes were taking things out of the fridge, and while Rikar was pretty sure they didn't need sausages for the pancakes, Samara could eat whatever she wanted. Rikar wouldn't care even if she emptied the fridge.

"She's dealing with it," he told Win. "She didn't sleep great, but I expected it."

Win sighed. "I can only imagine what they went through."

"I don't *want* to imagine it." Rikar needed to be there for Samara, not to make things worse for both of them, and he would if he obsessed over that.

"Well, I'm calling you about her."

Rikar's stomach turned to lead. Even though he and Samara had only met yesterday, he liked the little girl. He wanted to keep her safe, to make her happy, even though it didn't make much sense. What also didn't make much sense was that he wanted to keep her, but he did.

"We've been looking through the documents we found in the lab and researching these kids. We've already found a few families, but Samara doesn't have anyone left."

"She told me her mother left."

"I'm not sure exactly what happened, but I can tell you what I found in her file."

"Please. I need to know."

Win didn't ask him why he needed to know. Rikar was glad because he didn't have an answer.

"Her father died when she was two. I'm not sure what happened, but the file said that he was working in a factory. That left her alone with her mother, but that didn't last long. Her mother struggled, and eventually, she just left. There's a note in the file that a neighbor found Samara crying in the hallway of their apartment building when she was five. She couldn't find Samara's mother, so she called social services. They weren't able to locate her, either, and Samara's grandparents on her mother's side refused to take her in. Her grandparents on her father's side are dead, so she ended up in foster care. She was moved from home to home, never settling in. Then one day, she just never came back from school. They thought she'd run away."

"But she was kidnapped."

"Yes. That was a year ago."

Rikar wanted to kill someone. Samara had been in that lab, in that *cage*, for a year?

He looked up to watch her and Hayes work together on the pancakes. He didn't think Hayes had any experience with children, but it was good to see that he was including Samara.

She kept some distance from him, clearly still wary, but she didn't hesitate to give him tips or to order him around. Watching them made Rikar wonder if he could have this—if they could be a family.

He wanted them to. It wouldn't be easy, but it didn't matter. Hayes and Samara were two people he wanted in his life, in his home, and he was ready to do pretty much anything to get that.

"So she doesn't have anyone to go back to," Win continued. "If we can't find someone else, she'd have to go back to foster care."

"She can stay with me," Rikar said. He didn't have to think about it.

"I was hoping you'd say that. Are you sure, though? She's not only a ten-year-old without a family. She went through things that she might never be able to recover from, at least not mentally. Raising her won't be easy."

"I don't care about that." And Rikar truly didn't. His future was in front of him, quietly talking to each other and making pancakes. How could he refuse? How could he not offer to take care of Samara and create a family with her and Hayes?

Hayes kept an eye on Samara as he tried to listen to the conversation Rikar was having. He couldn't be sure who Rikar was talking to, but he had a good idea, considering what Rikar was saying.

He wanted to keep Samara.

Hayes didn't blame him. He also wanted to keep the girl, and she wasn't even living with him. He couldn't begin to imagine what her life had been like, and he didn't want it to be even harder. She deserved a family and a safe place to call home, and Rikar could give her that.

But that meant that Hayes would have to be involved, too.

Was he ready to have a child?

He considered that question as he and Samara cooked pancakes together, along with the sausages she'd found in the fridge. He'd never been great with babies, but Samara wasn't a baby. She was a ten-year-old, and even though she came with challenges, she was old enough to be independent. Hayes had no doubt that raising her would still be tough, but she was at an age where they could hopefully reason with her. None of this would be easy, but maybe, it would be easier if he and Rikar faced it together.

Samara was a sweetheart who'd been through hell — a hell no one should go through. Hayes couldn't do anything to fix her past and to make her forget what had happened to her, but he could do everything in his power to make sure her future would be a happy one. Besides, who better than he could understand her?

The experiences of the people who'd been kidnapped and experimented on in the labs differed, but some were similar. Hayes had been through what Samara was going through now, and maybe he could help her deal with everything.

Rikar hung up as Hayes put the first plate on the table. Samara had wanted two pancakes and two sausages, and he watched as she grabbed the maple syrup and drenched everything on her plate with it. His teeth hurt just looking at it, but he could tell she hadn't been given much to eat lately, so she needed this.

"Sorry for that," Rikar said as he came closer.

"Not a problem. What do you want on your plate?"

"Three pancakes and one sausage, please."

Hayes grinned at him. "You have a sweet tooth?"

"More than one."

Instead of sitting at the table with Samara, Rikar took the plate and leaned back against the counter. He used a fork to spear his sausage and take a bite, chewing as he watched the girl eat. "I'm sorry I didn't ask what you wanted to do," he said.

Hayes didn't understand what he was talking about. "You mean about breakfast?"

"No, about Samara. I know you heard at least part of my conversation with Win."

"You mean when you said you were keeping her."

Rikar nodded, a frown appearing on his face. "Win told me that she doesn't have anyone else. If I don't take her in, he'll have to find someone else who can, or she'll be sent back to foster care."

It wasn't unheard of to have shifter children in human foster care, but it also wasn't common. Often, humans either didn't want to deal with what having a shifter child meant or were just plain afraid. It was ridiculous, but Hayes supposed he couldn't know everyone's situation. He suspected that if it came to that, the council would find a shifter family who could adopt Samara.

But they wouldn't need to.

He leaned closer. "I have no problems with you adopting Samara."

"Are you sure? Because you never asked for any of this. If I adopt her, it means she'll be in your life as much as she's in mine, at least if we're together."

Hayes swallowed. "Aren't we?"

Rikar stared at him for a moment before a smile appeared on his lips. "Do you want us to be?"

"I wouldn't be here if I didn't want you in my life. This is going fast, maybe too much for me, but I'm clinging to the knowledge that you're my mate and that you won't hurt me." And it wasn't just because of the bond. It was because Rikar was a good person through and through.

"I'll try my best not to," Rikar confirmed. "Which is why I should have asked you what you thought about me adopting

Samara."

"You want to know what I think about it? I think that she needs a home and a loving family. She deserves someone to take care of her and make sure that she's happy for the rest of her life. She clearly wants to stay with you, and I think that in a way, she already loves you.

"I can't think of a better person to take her in permanently because you keep her safe and make her happy. You'll make the hard decisions and deal with the nightmares and everything else."

Hayes wished he'd had someone to do the same for him after he'd been freed from the lab, but he'd been an adult. He could have gone home and stayed with his parents, and he almost had. He would have if the mutants hadn't stepped in and Moore hadn't contacted him. Thanks to him, Hayes had a family who understood and loved him, and he'd met his best friend. He'd never thought he would leave them, but maybe it was time to expand his life. There was a place in it both for the mutants and for Rikar and Samara. Besides, the mutants lived in town now. Even if Hayes moved into Rikar's home, he wouldn't be far.

They sat at the table with Samara, who was already almost done eating. She barely glanced at them, too focused on her food. There was maple syrup around her mouth, making her skin glisten, and Hayes reached for a napkin before he could think of it. He used it to clean Samara's mouth as she stared at him, her dark eyes wide but with no trace of fear.

Could Hayes do this? Could he settle down with Rikar and help him raise Samara?

He didn't know the answer to that question, but he could see himself doing it. It was a lot to take in at once, but he didn't want to give up on Rikar or Samara. It would take time for them to learn how to be with each other and become a family, but that was okay. They had time. Rikar didn't expect Hayes to want to bond with him right away, though Hayes couldn't deny it was something he was starting to consider. They needed to spend more time together, and with Samara, they probably wouldn't be able to go out on a date.

Or they could take her with them.

Hayes didn't know what would happen next, but he did know that he wanted to find out, and the only way for him to do so was to stick around and become part of Samara and Rikar's lives. The thought would have terrified him a few weeks ago, but now, he found himself *wanting* that. It would be the best way for the three of them to get to know each other and decide whether or not they could do this.

"Are you going to adopt me?" Samara suddenly asked.

She was looking at Rikar, but Hayes found himself holding his breath anyway.

Rikar put down his fork, used a napkin to clean his mouth, and took his time to answer. "Is that something you'd like?" he asked cautiously.

Samara's eyes narrowed. "I know I'm too old to be adopted."

"Who said that?"

She shrugged, trying to look as if she didn't care, but it was obvious she did. "Everyone. They said that people want babies, not girls like me."

"Well, that's not true for me. I don't want a baby, and neither does Hayes, at least not for now. What we want is a little girl who's as smart and brave as you. As long as you don't have any other family or anyone you want to live with, I'd like to adopt you. You can say no, of course."

Samara blinked. "You want me?" she asked, her voice trembling slightly.

Once again, Hayes's heart broke for her. Maybe raising a child wasn't the best way to start a relationship or the best reason to decide to have one, but Hayes didn't care. Samara needed love, and he had plenty of that to give her. He also wanted Rikar more than he'd ever wanted anyone else.

Why would the reason for them to be together matter? They were made for each other, after all.

Once again, Rikar wanted to find everyone who'd ever hurt Samara and kill them. Instead, he focused on the little girl who looked like she was about to start crying. "I do want you."

"I'm going to be your daughter?"

"If you want. I realize you haven't known me long, and I wouldn't be offended if you decided you'd rather go somewhere else or if you want someone else to become your parent."

Samara shook her head. "I don't want anyone else. You saved me."

"Many people worked with me to take you out of that lab."

"But I don't want those people. I want to stay with you."

Rikar smiled. "Then you'll stay." He'd fight whoever tried taking Samara away from him. There was no reason to give her to someone else when she didn't have a family.

Samara sobbed once, then scrambled out of her chair. Rikar was ready for her when she threw herself into his arms, having moved his chair away from the table. She climbed into his lap, and he held her as she cried against his neck.

He looked at Hayes. He wanted his mate to be a part of his and Samara's life and their future. They'd have to talk about things, and it wouldn't be easy, but Rikar knew they could do it. He couldn't imagine a future where he didn't have Samara and Hayes.

But Hayes hadn't rejected Rikar. He hadn't stepped back when Rikar had said he wanted Samara. Instead, he was smiling with a soft expression that told Rikar everything he wanted to know. He wished he could feel Hayes's emotions, but in the meantime, watching him smile like this was enough.

Rikar reached for Hayes, and Hayes took his hand and linked their fingers together. He squeezed, nodding at Rikar. "We'll be a family," he whispered.

Rikar's chest felt too tight for the amount of emotion in it. "We will," he whispered back.

In the end, that was all that mattered.

Once Samara wasn't crying anymore, Rikar gently guided her back to her seat, where she finished eating. She got two more pancakes, wolfing them down as if she hadn't already eaten two of them and two sausages. Rikar needed to go grocery shopping, and he and Hayes had to buy everything Samara needed. They had so many things to do that it was overwhelming, but looking at Hayes and Samara talking as they ate was enough to help Rikar calm down.

"Go and wash up," he told Samara once she was done eating. "I'll grab you a clean t-shirt of mine that you can wear once you're done, but we'll have to go grocery shopping and get you clothes."

She nodded. "Can I come?"

"You have to, because I have no idea what you need, and I want you to choose your things."

She looked down at herself. "I can't wear your t-shirt to go to the store."

That much was true, and Rikar hadn't thought about it. "I'll think of something. We don't have to go right this moment, so you have enough time to wash up. Off you go."

Samara huffed and her expression turned stubborn, giving Rikar a peek of what their future would be like. It made him smile instead of terrifying him because he knew he wouldn't face it on his own.

Once Samara had disappeared down the hallway—after

Rikar asked her to go twice more—he turned to Hayes. "You're sure you want to do this? Because she'll be a terrifying teenager."

"I've never been more sure of anything, and I had an idea."

"What is it?"

"Well, my brother is a family lawyer. I know the council will probably take care of everything, but I thought we could bring him in, too. He can help us make everything official for the government, especially if he works with the council. We should call him anyway. Finding homes for all the kids who don't have a family won't be easy, and we'll need help."

Rikar felt he was responsible for the children who now lived with his tribe. He was ready to work with anyone who could help him, and this way, he'd have the opportunity to get to know Hayes's brother.

"Call anyone you want," he said. "If they can help the children, I'll be more than happy to meet them."

Hayes's smile was blinding. "I'll let him know. He's going to want to meet you, especially after I tell him I'm your mate."

"Then I'll meet him. Or did you want to keep me a secret?"

"Never." Hayes leaned over the table. "I have no idea what I'm doing, but I know I want this."

"As do I." Rikar didn't think he'd ever wanted anything more, and he was afraid to trust this.

Was it really possible that he'd found both his mate and a child in such a short time? He'd always believed he was too busy and too focused on the tribe to be able to have a family, but now he did. It would take some time getting used to, and he'd have to work hard to make sure neither Hayes nor Samara felt neglected, but he felt ready for the challenge.

"Where should we start?" Hayes asked.

"With what?"

"Well, everything. We need to talk to the council about this adoption thing and about my brother. We have to buy everything Samara needs and find her a therapist. I'm sure Rocco will want to see her again, just to check up on her, but it might not be a bad thing to find her a doctor in town, maybe someone used to dealing with the labs. I also have to talk to my mother and tell her that I'm not coming home and that I'm in a relationship and we have a child."

Hayes was talking too fast, almost as if he was panicking. Rikar didn't blame him and agreed that they needed to do all those things. First, though, he had one question to ask.

He squeezed Hayes's hand hard enough to get Hayes's attention. Hayes stopped talking, giving Rikar the occasion to say what was on his mind.

"I think that first, we should decide what's going on between us. I don't want to confuse Samara, although that's not the main reason I want to know."

"What's the main reason, then?"

"You're my mate, and I want to know if you'll be in my future."

Hayes stared for a moment. "Of course I will. How can I not want everything you're offering?" Hayes sniffled and looked away. "You know, I was convinced I'd end up alone. I can't go back to my old life with my family, but as a human, sometimes, I feel like I don't quite fit with the mutants. All of us have abilities, but they're also shifters and paranormal creatures, while I'm just me."

"Just you is perfect."

Hayes's smile was wobbly. "For you, maybe."

Rikar raised Hayes's hand and kissed its back. "Isn't that all that matters? I want you, Hayes. I want anything you can give me right now and everything you'll be able to give me in the future. I want us and Samara to be a family, to work through our problems together. I realize it won't be easy and that you're still dealing with what happened to you in the labs as much as Samara is, but I've always been up for a challenge.

I wouldn't want another mate, and I hope you know that."

"You weren't so sure in the beginning."

And that was a mistake, but it was a mistake Rikar was still in time to fix. "I've always wanted you, since the first time I saw you. I just didn't know how to tell you and how to fit you in my life, but I shouldn't have worried, because it's as if you've always been part of it."

"I feel I've always known you," Hayes murmured.

"That's because our hearts and our souls recognized each other. They don't care about our doubts and what's going on around us. They just want to be together."

"I agree with them."

It was too soon to ask Hayes to bond, but the thought was in the back of Rikar's mind. Eventually, he'd ask, but for now, this was more than enough to make him happy.

Hayes was more than enough to make him happy.

CHAPTER FIVE

Hayes couldn't avoid it anymore. His mother had been calling him repeatedly, and no matter how many times he told her he was busy, she kept bringing up the fact that he promised he'd come to dinner.

And he *had* promised. If he was going to raise Samara with Rikar, he needed to be a good example for her. That meant keeping promises. She needed to know he always would after what she'd been through, and he never wanted to disappoint her or Rikar.

It was odd how easily Hayes had taken to having a mate and a daughter. He wasn't living with them yet, but he spent all of his free time at the house, and he wouldn't have it any other way. They needed to sort things out before he could move in with them, including the fact that he and Rikar weren't bonded yet, but they would. They just needed to give it time.

Time Hayes didn't have any more when it came to his mother.

Rikar kissed Hayes's temple. "You'll be fine, and so will we."

"I just don't see why I should go, especially without the two of you."

"You're going because you love your mother and promised her you'd go."

He was right, and while Hayes was whining, he had every intention of going. Even though his mother was pushy, she meant well and loved him. He missed her when he didn't see her, and he was looking forward to talking to her and eating some of the great food she cooked. Hayes didn't exactly suck in the kitchen, but he also wasn't great at cooking. Hopefully, he'd be able to bring leftovers back to Rikar and Samara.

Samara was curled on the couch, watching Hayes and Rikar. She did that often, and in the first few days, Hayes had wondered if it was because she was afraid of them. He'd realized she was just intrigued by the relationship between him and Rikar. They'd told her they were mates, but they'd also explained that they weren't bonded yet and were still working things out.

"Do you think I'll ever meet your family?" she asked.

"Definitely." In any other situation, Hayes would bring Rikar and Samara. As it was, both he and Rikar had agreed it would be better for Samara to have some time to get used to the situation she was in before meeting new people.

She was doing great, or at least as well as she could, considering everything. They'd gone shopping, and she'd turned one of the two guestrooms into her room. It had been simple and neat before, but now, it looked like a pink and purple bomb had exploded in it. Hayes was bewildered every time he peeked in, which wasn't often because he and Rikar were trying to give her as much space as she needed.

She also had a therapist. The woman had worked with several of the people the tribe had rescued from the labs over the years, so she knew what to expect. The first few sessions had been tough, but Samara was slowly relaxing with her, too, which was great. She needed to trust the therapist almost as much as she needed to trust Rikar and Hayes.

Rikar poked Hayes's ribs. "You should go."

Hayes groaned, but he got to his feet, then offered Rikar his hand. Thankfully, his mate had agreed to shimmer him to his parents' house. That way he wouldn't have to use one of the apps, and it would give him just a little bit more time with

Rikar. He wouldn't be away from Samara for long, and when they'd both tried to reassure her, she'd waved them off and told them that she was ten, so she could be on her own in the house for a few seconds.

Hayes hoped that was true.

Rikar allowed Hayes to pull him to his feet. Hayes then turned to Samara, bending over to kiss her forehead. She wrinkled her nose, but he could see she was pleased.

They were still trying to find their way around each other, and it was especially tough because Hayes didn't live here, which meant Samara and Rikar shared things he wasn't a part of. Sometimes he was jealous, but he understood the need for Samara not to be overwhelmed. Besides, the fact that he didn't live here yet didn't change much. He still spent every evening here, and while he hadn't spent the night yet, he hoped that he would soon. Being with Rikar was great, and kissing him was an experience Hayes had never thought possible, but he felt it was time for more.

His dick agreed with that.

After saying goodbye to Samara, Hayes headed to the porch. Rikar was right behind him, holding out his hand as soon as they arrived. Hayes sighed, then took it. "Next time, the two of you are coming with me," he said.

Rikar laughed and pulled him into his arms. "I promise we will. But tonight, you need to talk to your family and inform them of our presence in your life and of what happened to Samara."

It was one more reason Hayes was doing this on his own. He wanted his family to be aware of what Samara had gone through, and it wouldn't be right to talk about in front of her. This way, he'd be able to answer every question his family had about Samara and her experiences without having to keep himself in check.

"I'll tell them everything Samara is okay with me telling,"

he promised.

Rikar kissed his forehead. "I know you will."

He kissed him again, on the lips this time, and shimmered them in front of the home where Hayes had grown up in that position. Before Hayes could deepen the kiss, he stepped away, winked, then disappeared again, abandoning Hayes on the porch.

The door opened almost instantly, as if Hayes's mother had been waiting for him just behind it. She beamed when she saw him, and he couldn't help but smile back. Every time he came, it was like coming home, yet not.

"You're finally here!" she exclaimed, opening her arms.

Hayes stepped into them, closing his eyes at the familiarity of the hug. As reluctant as he was to visit his mom, coming here was still comfortable. "I told you I'd come eventually."

"It's the *eventually* I didn't like. It took you too long."

"I have work to do."

"I know, but come in. I have a surprise for you."

Hayes's stomach suddenly churned. His mother's surprises were never good, like that time for his ninth birthday when she'd hired a clown even though he was terrified of them.

He still was.

He followed his mother inside, and she closed the door behind him, almost as if she were afraid he'd run away. The joke was on her because he could fly or contact his mate if he needed to leave. She didn't know about Rikar yet, and Hayes didn't want to dump all of this in her lap immediately.

"Everyone is in the kitchen having drinks," she said, leading the way.

"Everyone?"

Hayes got the answer to his question before his mother could say anything when he walked into the kitchen. His brother was at the counter, sipping on something dark and talking to their father. There was another man, and Hayes's stomach dropped at seeing his ex-boyfriend.

Their relationship had been good, but they'd been together when Hayes had been kidnapped, and Benedict had been seeing someone else when he came back. Hayes had been hurt, even though logically, he hadn't expected Benedict to wait for him when he didn't even know if Hayes was alive. Benedict was a great guy, and he deserved to be happy. After what Hayes had gone through, he couldn't be the person Benedict needed, so he'd agreed it would be better for them to stay apart. They'd only dated for a little over six months, and while they might have had a future before, they didn't anymore.

So why was Benedict here?

Hayes turned to his mother.

"I just thought that seeing Benedict would show you that you still have a life to come back to," she quickly said. She could probably see the anger in Hayes's expression.

"What are you talking about?"

"I know you always say that you have a job and a life, but you can have both those things here. You can have *more*. You could come back to your old life, and I already talked to your old boss, and he said you could have your job back. Benedict is single right now, and he was excited to see you again. Everything is just like you left it. We just need you to come home."

"Were you listening when I told you I couldn't? My old life might still be in place, but I'm not the same, Mom. I changed, and there's no coming back from what was done to me."

She winced. "You could act normal. You're still human, and as long as you keep your feet on the ground, no one is going to know you're different."

Hayes had to resist the urge to scream. Had his mother been listening to him when they talked on the phone? He didn't know how often he'd told her he couldn't just return to his old life, but she didn't seem to have understood.

Or maybe she had, but she didn't care.

Rikar was supposed to focus on the movie he and Samara were watching — there was magic and a house where a big family lived — but it was almost impossible. His thoughts kept drifting to Hayes and what he was doing, and it was tempting to shimmer back to the home where he'd taken Hayes to check on him. Hayes had been conflicted about visiting his family, but Rikar had pushed him to go. He wasn't afraid Hayes would change his mind and decide to stay there permanently. Hayes had told him that he and Samara were a family now, and Rikar trusted him.

"Why aren't you and Hayes bonded?" Samara suddenly asked. She was still staring at the TV, but her mind was clearly somewhere else, like Rikar's.

"Because we haven't known each other long."

She twisted on the couch, tucking one of her legs under her and facing Rikar. "Are you sure it's not because of me?"

She'd been doing that a lot, which the therapist said was normal. Samara had been abandoned once already, and she was terrified of being abandoned again. It didn't matter how many times Hayes and Rikar explained to her they'd never do something like that. She needed to be reassured, and Rikar was more than happy to do that.

He paused the movie and mirrored Samara's position so they could look each other in the eyes. "It's not because of you," he told her, putting as much conviction as he could in his voice. "It's because we haven't known each other long and because of what Hayes went through."

"The labs."

Rikar nodded. "I know that most of the time it doesn't look

like it, but Hayes is still struggling with some of the things that happened to him."

"It was awful."

It had been. Hayes and Samara had conversations about the labs and what had been done to them, and Rikar wasn't privy to them. He hadn't gone through the same experiences, and he wanted them to have their privacy. There were things the two of them could only tell each other, and that was fine. Rikar didn't need to be the entirety of Hayes's and Samara's lives. They needed to have each other, too, and they did.

"That's why he's seeing your therapist, too."

He'd only started after they'd brought Samara to her, so it was recent, but Rikar hoped it would help both of them. They were the most important people in his life, and he needed them to be okay. He'd be their rock, their lighthouse in the darkness, the home they could always come back to when they needed to, but unfortunately, they were the only ones who could do the work on themselves.

"But you'll bond eventually, right? And we'll be a real family?"

"Aren't we already a family?"

"Well, yeah, but I want Hayes and you to bond."

"Why?"

Samara shrugged and looked away. "I guess I just want two dads."

Rikar leaned forward, careful to go slow so he wouldn't spook Samara. Physically, she was the most comfortable with him, and she didn't resist when he pulled her into a hug. She buried her face against his neck like she always did, and he held her and breathed in her scent.

"You already have two dads," he murmured. "The fact that Hayes and I aren't bonded yet doesn't change that. We both love you very much, and that's never going to change." He could feel there was something else there, but he didn't know how to get to it without pushing too much.

"What if he leaves?" Samara asked so softly that he almost didn't hear it.

So she was afraid Hayes would leave because he and Rikar weren't bonded. "Why would he?"

"Because of me. Maybe I'll be the reason the two of you don't bond."

"Hayes knew what he was getting into when he decided to be with me." Rikar stroked Samara's hair. "He loves you as much as I do, which shouldn't be possible, considering we've only known you a few weeks. But we do, and neither of us wants to give you up. Your presence in my life isn't going to push Hayes away. If anything, I think it'll make him want to be with me even more. He's already been talking about moving in with us, and I think that maybe it's time."

Samara leaned away and grinned. "Really?"

"We'll have to talk to him about it, but yes." It didn't make sense for Hayes to spend the evenings with him and Samara, then return to the home he shared with the other mutants. He wanted to stay, and Rikar and Samara wanted him to do so. Why were they torturing themselves this way?

Samara's smile was beautiful. "I promise I won't bother you in your bedroom when the door is closed," she said.

Rikar laughed, although he wondered if that was something she should know already. He and Hayes were going to need help when it came to raising Samara. "I'm sure you won't."

His phone vibrated, and even though it was too early for Hayes to be ready to come home, Rikar checked the screen after pushing play on the movie again. Even though he had a family now, he was still the tribe leader, and he had to deal with all the problems that came with it. Luckily, everyone knew about Samara, and they were understanding when he couldn't drop everything to get to them as soon as they needed help.

But it was Hayes.

Rikar frowned and opened the text. He wasn't sure what to expect, but it wasn't for Hayes to ask him to come as soon as possible. That was all Hayes had written, and it made Rikar worry. Was his mate in trouble? He was supposed to be having dinner with his family, so it didn't make sense, but why had he texted that?

"Samara, is it okay if I leave you alone for a bit?"

"Is it work?" she asked.

"Yes. I have to solve a problem, but I'll be as fast as possible."

She settled back against the couch, turning her attention back to the movie. "I'm ten. I can be alone."

Rikar had no doubt about that, and he wasn't worried about her making messes or doing something she shouldn't. No, the main problem with her was that he didn't want her to feel abandoned. He couldn't take her with him, though. He had no idea what he'd be shimmering into.

"Are you sure?" he asked as he put his shoes on.

"I'm sure. You don't have to worry about me. I'm not a baby."

Rikar didn't push. Instead, he bent down to kiss her forehead, then shimmered away. He focused on Hayes so he'd get to him immediately, and he appeared in a kitchen. It looked normal, with food cooking on the stove, brightly lit, and a set table by a window.

A woman screeched when Rikar appeared. Rikar winced, but she wasn't his main focus. No, that was Hayes, who was facing the woman and was angry. His jaw was set, and his hands were bunched into fists, almost as if he was going to fight her physically. Three men were at the counter, staring, and they started freaking out as soon as Rikar appeared.

Hayes raised a hand. "This is Rikar," he said. "I asked him

to come."

The woman pressed a hand over her heart. "Why? What's going on?"

Hayes's eyes were narrow. He grabbed Rikar's hand and linked their fingers together, and the woman's eyes widened. "When I told you I wasn't coming home, I wasn't lying," Hayes said. "I don't know why you didn't listen to me, or if you listened and decided you didn't care about what I wanted and needed, but you should have. It's not just that I can't come back to my old life, Mom. I also have a new life, and I don't want to leave it behind."

So the woman was Hayes's mother. That made sense since Hayes had been headed to dinner with her and the rest of his family.

Rikar looked at the men. One was older, and was no doubt Hayes's father, and one of the other two had to be Hayes's brother. But what about the last one? Who was he?

"But your life was here," Hayes's mother protested. "And your family still is. Don't you want to be normal again? Why do you have to do those things you do, raid the labs and put yourself in danger for people you don't know?"

"Because no one else will. Because if someone hadn't put themselves in danger even though they didn't know me, I wouldn't be standing here today," Hayes told her. "Because it's the right thing to do, and I want to do it." He swallowed heavily. "And since you don't seem to understand that, we need to talk, and this time, you'll *have* to listen to me."

Rikar had no idea what was happening, although what Hayes's mother had just said gave him a hint. It was clear Hayes and his family were about to have a conversation he wanted Rikar to be there for, and while it was unexpected, Rikar was more than happy to support him.

It was one of the things mates were there for, after all.

Hayes didn't know where to start. He wanted to yell at his mother, but he reminded himself that while she'd walked all over what he'd told her, she was doing it because she cared about him and wanted him to be happy. Right now, though, it was hard to remember that.

"Maybe we should sit down," Rikar suggested.

"I don't think I can sit down."

"Maybe not, but your mother looks like she should sit."

"Who are you?" Hayes's brother Lucas asked, stepping forward.

Hayes raised the hand he wasn't using to clutch Rikar's. "I promise I'll explain everything, including who Rikar is. Can you just give me a moment to breathe?"

Lucas looked guilty. "Of course. I'm sorry I didn't tell you about this. Mom said you were happy to come back."

Hayes was starting to see that his mom had said and done many things she shouldn't have. "I was happy to come back for *dinner*, but I'm not moving back. I have a new home, and while you guys will always be my family, you're not the most important people in my life anymore."

A sob escaped Hayes's mother, and she pressed a hand to her mouth. Hayes's father stepped in, looking worried, but not like he blamed Hayes for what was happening. Hayes was relieved, because he didn't want his father to be angry at him. He just wanted his mother to listen.

His father wrapped an arm around his mother's shoulders and guided her toward the table. Benedict moved fast, pulling out a chair so she could sit. Once he was done, though, he looked awkward and like he shouldn't be there, which was the case. Hayes couldn't blame him for being at this dinner, though. He doubted his mother had told Benedict everything there was to know about the situation.

Rikar gently squeezed Hayes's hand. "All right?" he asked.

"I don't know, but we're about to find out."

"I can stay if you want, but remember who's at home."

Hayes didn't want to leave Samara alone for long, so he needed to get a move on.

He cleared his throat. He wanted to cling to Rikar, but he needed to do this on his own, so he let go of Rikar's hand and moved closer to his family. Lucas went to sit in front of their mother on the other side of the table, and the three of them, plus Benedict, stared.

"I know you mean well," Hayes told his mother. "And I know you miss me and feel like you lost me twice. You were terrified when I was kidnapped, and when I reappeared, you thought I'd be coming home and acting as if nothing had changed, but I can't do that when everything has."

Hayes's father nodded while Hayes's mother cried. It hurt to see her like this, but this was a conversation they should have had a while ago. Hayes had avoided it because he didn't want to hurt anyone, least of all his mom, but now he could see he'd been wrong. He should have been honest with her from the beginning.

He supposed he had been, though. He'd told her that he'd decided to stay back and help the mutants rescue other people from the labs. He'd told her he had a new home and that the other mutants felt like a whole other family.

But she'd still hoped, and Hayes couldn't avoid thinking that maybe it was because of something he'd done or said.

"I'm not entirely human anymore," he said. "I can't ignore that when I can use my ability to help other people. And I know you think it's not my business, but it is. I wouldn't be here today if it weren't for the people who saved me. I want to help others just like they did, and I want to close all the labs. They shouldn't exist, but since no one is doing much about them, we are. We're saving people, and I don't want to stop doing it." Especially when they saved children like

Samara. Maybe his mother would understand better once he mentioned her.

"But you could be hurt," his mother said. "I could lose you again, and for good this time."

"I realize that, but this is something only I can decide. I hate that you feel this way, but even if I didn't work with the mutants anymore, I still wouldn't be moving home because I have a life there. Besides, I also have problems I haven't told you about. I have nightmares, and I just started seeing a therapist. She thinks I have PTSD, which honestly isn't surprising. But I wake up during the night screaming and crying, and I don't want you to have to live through that. It's bad enough that I do." He clung to Rikar's hand as he flung himself off the cliff. "But anyway, as I mentioned before, this is Rikar. He's my mate."

For one second, no one said anything. They all stared, and Hayes held his breath, wondering what they would all say. Then his father's shoulders relaxed, and his mother smiled. Lucas grinned at him, and that was all Hayes needed.

"You have a mate?" his mother asked.

"Rikar is the leader of the tribe with which the mutants live. He's one of the reasons I call it home."

His mother rubbed her cheeks, probably trying to get rid of any sign that she'd been crying. "You should have told me."

"I wanted to, but we've been figuring things out. Besides, he's not the only big change in my life. The mutants recently rescued a group of children from one of those labs."

Someone sucked in a breath. Hayes was glad they found this horrifying, even though they hadn't seen the labs and what had been done to the children.

"I'm in the process of adopting one of those children," Rikar interjected. He looked at Lucas. "Hayes mentioned you might be able to help."

Lucas appeared nonplussed, but he nodded. "I definitely can look into it. I, uh, I guess congratulations on everything. I'm not sure what else to say."

Hayes grinned. "You don't have to say anything else." He turned back to his mother. "But now you have to see why I can't come back, right? It's not only that I don't have a life here and that I can't go back to what I lost when I was kidnapped. I'm happy where I am, and I don't want to lose Rikar and Samara."

His mother sniffed. "I just wanted my son back home. I want you to be safe and happy."

"And I am, even though it's not with you."

"Then I suppose it's all right. But you better introduce me to your daughter as soon as possible. I can't wait to spoil her."

Hayes laughed. He was glad his mother and the rest of the family seemed eager to accept Samara, but they still needed to have a conversation about her. "I'll introduce the two of you as soon as possible, but first, you should know what she's had to live through."

It was one of the hardest conversations Hayes had ever had. When it was over, he needed to breathe and take some time alone, so he headed to the back porch. He wasn't sure that leaving Rikar on his own with his family was a good idea, but Rikar was an adult. Besides, it wasn't like Hayes's family was going to eat him.

Hayes closed the kitchen door behind himself and leaned against the railing. He tilted his head to look at the sky and took a deep breath, then another. All in all, it had gone well, even though his mother had cried several times.

The door behind him opened again, and he almost groaned. He was both relieved and worried when he saw it was Benedict rather than his mother. He had no idea what to tell his ex. He'd thought he'd known where they both stood after he'd come back, but maybe that wasn't the case.

"You're happy," Benedict said.

It wasn't a question, but Hayes nodded. "I am. I never thought I could have any of this, and I'm glad I do."

Benedict's smile was wistful. "I'm glad you do, too. You deserve to be happy and to have someone who loves you."

"I don't know if it's love yet, but we're growing closer, and I really like Rikar."

"That's good. I'm sorry I ambushed you. Your mother said you knew I was coming."

"I'm not surprised. I'm sorry you were dragged into this."

Benedict stared at him for a moment. "It's fine. I missed you, and while I know we can't be together again, I'd like to be your friend."

Before, Hayes would have said no. It would have hurt too much. But now, with Rikar and Samara in his life and things finally going the way they should, he found himself nodding. "I'd like to be your friend."

Meeting Rikar and Samara had been a new beginning for Hayes, but maybe he didn't have to leave all of his past behind.

Rikar had no idea what to do. He was here for Hayes, but Hayes was outside with a man who seemed to be his blind date. Rikar wasn't jealous and had no intention of interrupting whatever was happening on the porch. Hayes was more than able to defend himself if he had to.

It seemed like Hayes's mother was more similar to Rikar's mothers than Rikar was expecting. That wasn't a bad thing, considering how much his mothers loved him. Everything Hayes's mother had done was for her son's sake, even though she'd made a mess.

Rikar cleared his throat. He didn't want to look uncomfortable, but he was. Hayes's parents and his brother were all staring at him as if he had two heads.

Thankfully, Hayes's brother seemed to realize what they were doing and decided to take pity on him. He smiled and moved closer, gesturing at the counter. "Can I get you anything to drink?"

"Water is fine."

"You're sure? We have stronger stuff, and you look like you could use it."

"Maybe, but I'm fine."

Lucas nodded and walked around the counter to get the water. Rikar followed him to the counter and sat on one of the stools. He could still feel Hayes's parents' gazes on his back, and they started whispering to each other, but as long as he didn't see them, he'd be fine.

"So, you want to adopt Samara?" Lucas asked.

Rikar was glad for the conversation opener. "Yes. I don't know why, but she got attached to me, and I don't want her to have to go back to the human foster system."

Lucas placed a glass full of water in front of Rikar, who nodded in thanks.

"The human foster system isn't great for shifter kids," Lucas said.

From what Rikar had heard, it wasn't great for any kids, but he didn't say that. "I'm not saying humans can't understand her or that they treat her badly because she's a shifter, but between that and what she's been through in the lab, I'd be more comfortable if she had a supernatural family."

"And from what Hayes said, she's already chosen you."

"I'm not sure why, but she latched onto me in the lab. I didn't make her any promises, but she wants to stay with me, and I'm ready to give her the best life I can. I'm the leader of my tribe and unofficial mayor of the town we settled in. It's growing a bit more every day, and it's not without complications, but Samara will be safe and able to live the way she deserves and wants."

Lucas raised his hands. "I don't doubt your ability and your desire to be a good father to her. In fact, I'll help you and the council any way I can."

Rikar was relieved. "Can I give you a friend's phone number? He works for the council, and they've been talking about how to best help the children for whom they hadn't been able to find a family. I don't know the story of all of them, but the council wants them to be safe, and they might need help."

Lucas's eyes widened. "I'd love to work for the council, although I have to admit I'm surprised they don't have their own lawyers."

"They probably do, but as I said, I don't know the entire situation. Win will be able to give you more details."

"And I'll be happy to listen."

A door opened behind Rikar, and he was glad to see Hayes was coming back inside. The other man was behind him, and they both seemed pleased and at peace. Hayes made a beeline for Rikar.

"Sorry I abandoned you. I needed a moment to breathe," he said.

Rikar smiled at him — how could he not? "I'm fine. Are you ready to go home? I don't want to leave Samara alone longer than I have to."

Hayes nodded and turned to his family. Rikar got up and stepped to the side to give them a moment to say goodbye. The man who'd been outside with Hayes shuffled his feet, clearly uncomfortable, so Rikar was surprised when he offered him his hand.

"I'm Benedict."

Rikar shook his hand. "Rikar, but you already know that."

"I do. And I'm sorry for all of this. I was told Hayes knew about everything and was ready to come home. I wouldn't have come if I'd known he had no idea I'd be there." He hesitated. "We were together for a while before he was kidnapped. We're not anymore, but I wanted to tell you so you'd be aware of everything. I have no intention of trying to get back with Hayes."

"I'm glad to hear that, but I wasn't worried."

Rikar was glad that Hayes was fixing things with his family, but he was glad when they were finally able to shimmer back home. Samara was curled up on the couch, waiting for them, and she scrambled to her feet when she saw them. She threw herself in Rikar's arms, then in Hayes's, and Rikar saw her visibly relax. She'd been dismissive when he left, but she'd clearly been worried.

"You're finally home!" she exclaimed.

Hayes patted her back. "And we're not leaving again. Now, shouldn't you be in bed already?"

Rikar found himself smiling. Hayes would be a good father — he already was. He didn't need Rikar to help him with Samara, and Samara obeyed when he told her to go brush her teeth.

She still had nightmares, but she was happy with her room and liked going to bed alone. More often than not, she ended up in bed with Rikar sometimes during the night, but Rikar didn't mind.

He was exhausted by the time Samara was asleep and more than ready for bed, but one glance from Hayes and his tiredness disappeared. There was something in Hayes's gaze that told Rikar something was about to happen, and while he didn't know what that something was, it didn't matter. Only Hayes did.

"Ready for bed?" Hayes asked.

"As long as you're coming with me."

Hayes smiled. "Always." He took Rikar's hand and pulled him down the hallway, away from Samara's bedroom.

He'd tell Rikar whatever was on his mind once he was

ready, so Rikar didn't ask. They got ready for bed, and he kept an ear open to ensure Samara was settled in her room. He couldn't hear anything, so once he'd washed up and used the bathroom, he slid into bed and waited for Hayes. When Hayes joined him, he turned off the light and pressed their bodies together. Rikar wrapped his arms around him and kissed the top of his head.

The silence of the house settled around them. Hayes was tense, and Rikar waited.

"How long do you think it will be before we bond?" Hayes eventually asked.

Rikar relaxed. If that was Hayes's problem, he could solve it. "Whenever you want. We don't have to wait if you're ready for it."

Hayes propped himself up on an elbow. He was only wearing his underwear, which exposed a whole lot of skin Rikar wanted to touch. It was the first time they'd shared a bed, but it wouldn't be the last—far from it—and they'd have to be careful. They'd mostly kept their hands to themselves until now. They were settling in their new shared life, and there was Samara to think about.

But tonight would be different. Rikar could tell.

"Isn't it too soon?" Hayes asked.

"Who gets to decide that? You and I, or everyone else?" Rikar couldn't see Hayes's expression in the darkness, but he didn't need to. He hooked a hand behind Hayes's neck and pulled him down to kiss him.

Hayes came easily. When their lips met, it felt like coming home, and Rikar never wanted it to end. He thought Hayes felt the same.

"I want to do it now," Hayes murmured as he straddled Rikar.

"Yes."

Hayes laughed. "It's that easy?"

"Why wouldn't it be? You're my mate. We were destined to be together, and there's nothing simpler than that."

Rikar grabbed one of Hayes's hands and pressed it to his chest, then pressed his over Hayes's heart. He still couldn't see him, but he would in a moment.

His palm lit up. The soft light made it so that Rikar could see Hayes and look him in the eyes as the bond between them opened up and their souls reached out to each other. Hayes's eyes were wide, but he didn't lean back or try to stop Rikar. He wanted this as much as Rikar did.

Their souls touched, recognized each other, and intertwined. Rikar had never felt like he was missing something, but now, he felt complete. Hayes was a part of him, and he always would be.

I love you, he told him through their bond.

Hayes made a strangled sound and dropped on top on Rikar. Rikar couldn't hear anything through their bond, and with the light from his hand gone, he couldn't see the mark on Hayes's chest, but he knew it was there.

Hayes kissed Rikar and at the same time, tried to push a hand in his underwear. Rikar laughed, happier than he could ever remember being. He raised his hips to give Hayes enough space to do what he wanted, and Hayes pushed his boxer briefs down his legs. Rikar wiggled until they slid lower, then hooked one of his feet into them and finished taking them off. By the time he was done, Hayes was trying to untangle himself from his own underwear, and Rikar was more than happy to help him. He wanted Hayes naked and for them to be one.

They already were, and they always would be.

Love you. Love you. Love you.

The litany in the back of Rikar's mind came from Hayes, but he doubted Hayes realized what he was projecting. It would take both of them some time to get used to each other's presence, although it would be more complicated for Hayes, who was human.

But they didn't need to solve this now. Rikar cupped his hand on the back of Hayes's head and kept him in place as he kissed him. Hayes's body slid down slightly until he was between Rikar's spread legs. Rikar hooked his feet around Hayes's legs and thrust his hips up. Hayes quickly got with the program and pushed back against Rikar.

Rikar didn't need anything more. Feeling Hayes move against him was perfection and the beginning of something that would flourish and grow. Their relationship was new, but they had all the time they needed.

They had forever.

Rikar's pleasure was fed by Hayes's, heightening it. Rikar could feel everything Hayes felt, which meant he knew when to move and what to do to make Hayes fall apart.

But the same went for Hayes.

He might not fully understand what he felt the way Rikar did, but he could still feel what Rikar felt. He knew how to touch him the way he preferred without Rikar having to say a word.

They fell apart in each other's arms, but being bonded meant they also put each other back together.

And that was all that mattered.

CHAPTER SIX

Hayes didn't have many things to move, but he was glad it was done. Now everything he owned was in Rikar's home, which was his, too.

It had felt odd to leave Jessup and the others behind. They'd been Hayes's entire life since he'd been rescued from the lab, and he almost felt like he was losing part of himself. He'd had to remind himself that they were just a few minutes by foot and that they'd see each other every day. Now that he and Rikar had talked things out and he knew what they were doing, he'd started mixing those two sides of his life, and his friends had come over to dinner last night. Things had been slightly awkward in the beginning, but Rikar was Hayes's mate, while Jessup and the others were Hayes's family. They had to get along, and they did.

His phone vibrated in his pocket, and he took it out to see that his mother was calling. He started putting it back into his pocket, but a hand on his wrist stopped him. Rikar gently extracted the phone from his fingers, then looked down at the screen.

"You're still avoiding her?" he asked.

Hayes huffed. "I can avoid her if I want to."

"Well, of course you can, but why should you? I thought you'd talked things out."

They had, yet at the same time, they hadn't. Hayes was still angry at her for pushing so hard for him to come home. He wasn't sure she entirely believed he wouldn't change his mind about Rikar and Samara, which made him uncomfortable. His brother and his father had welcomed Rikar into the family, but while his mother was eager to meet Samara, she'd been cold to Rikar, and Hayes hadn't liked that.

Rikar sighed. "You really need to talk to her."

"Have you talked to your mothers yet?"

The flash of guilt in Rikar's expression told Hayes he hadn't. Hayes almost laughed, but he understood that it was much easier to keep this kind of thing to themselves than to talk to their parents. Rikar's mothers didn't seem to be anything like Hayes's mom, but they were still moms.

"How about I go talk to them and tell them about you and Samara, but first, I shimmer you to your mother?" he asked.

Hayes wanted to say no, but he also wanted Rikar to tell his mothers about him and Samara. It was starting to get awkward not to tell them because they lived in the same town. "Fine," he said. "But I'm not happy about this."

"And I have no doubt that you'll remind me of it again and again so I don't forget." There was humor in Rikar's tone. "But I want Samara to have a family. I want her to have grandmothers, and for that to happen, you need to get along with your mom. I'm not saying you need to accept what she did or to forgive her, but I do believe you need to clear things up."

"I did that at dinner."

"Not exactly. You told her about Samara and me, explained what Samara's gone through, then basically ordered me to shimmer you home. Your mom needed time to wrap her mind around everything and finally accept that you weren't coming back while you needed time for your anger to simmer down. Now that both of you have had a few days to sleep on it, I think it's time for you to talk and to be honest with her. Tell her she hurt you but that you want to fix the relationship."

"You're way too smart for me," Hayes said.

"That's not possible. You're my mate, which means I'm

perfect for you."

Hayes rolled his eyes, but he was glad that when he leaned against Rikar, Rikar took his weight. He'd never have to walk alone again. Whatever happened with his family or the other mutants, Rikar was the one person Hayes was never going to lose.

He did want Samara to have a good relationship with his mom. Samara had lost so much in her short life, and Hayes wanted to give her back everything. Giving her a family wasn't the easiest, but at least Hayes had one. Samara would be loved, and he didn't want to keep that from her just because he was angry.

"What about Samara?" he asked.

"I'll take her with me and introduce her to my mothers," Rikar told him before kissing the tip of his nose. "They'll want to see her as soon as I tell them about her, anyway. I might as well anticipate it."

"Won't Samara be overwhelmed?"

"Possibly, but I'll make sure my mothers know not to crowd her, and as soon as she wants to come home, we'll shimmer back. You don't have to worry. I'll keep her safe."

"I never doubted that."

It took the three of them a few moments to get ready. Samara was visibly nervous about meeting two of her grandmothers, but both Rikar and Hayes reassured her that everything would be okay. It would be impossible for anyone not to fall in love with the girl, as they knew well. They'd fallen for her so quickly and thoroughly that they were adopting her.

Rikar shimmered Hayes in front of his parents' house. The three of them stood there, staring at the door for a moment.

"Let me know if I need to pick you up," Rikar murmured.

"I'll let you know as soon as I'm ready to come home. I don't think this is going to be as bad as it was the other night, though."

"She already knows about Samara and me, so you don't need to tell her about us. You just need to talk to her."

The problem was that Hayes had tried several times, and his mother hadn't listened. What was to say she would this time around? She'd seemed to accept that he wasn't coming home, but he wasn't sure she had, and they needed to clear the air between them, as little as he was looking forward to it.

He waited until Rikar and Samara had both kissed his cheek and shimmered away to knock on the door. His father would be at work at this time of day, which meant he'd have time to talk things through with his mom without anyone interrupting them.

He heard footsteps, and since he didn't want his mom to think something was wrong, he plastered a smile on his face. She looked surprised when she opened, but she scowled at him right away.

"Why are you knocking on the door of your home?" she demanded to know.

"It's not my home anymore. I don't live here."

"You don't have to remind me every time you see me."

This wasn't going well, but while it would be easy for Hayes to contact Rikar and demand he come pick him up, he'd made a promise. He needed to fix this, and he needed to do it today. "I'm not here to fight with you," he said.

She looked hesitant, but she stepped aside. "Let's go to the kitchen."

The smells of the house were familiar, and they soothed something in Hayes, even though he was still nervous. He didn't want to lose his mom, but if he had to choose between his mother and the family he was creating with Rikar and Samara, she'd always come second. That would have been the case even if Hayes hadn't met Rikar but rather married Benedict.

"Has something happened?" she asked when they reached the kitchen.

She started making tea, which was another reminder of Hayes's childhood. When someone had a problem or needed to talk things through, she sat them down and gave them tea.

"Well, Rikar and I bonded," he said.

She almost dropped the mug she'd been taking out of the cupboard. "Already? Didn't you tell me you haven't met that long ago?"

"I did, and we haven't, but he's it for me. We're mates, and while it doesn't mean as much for me as it does for him, it does mean something to me, too. I've always known he wouldn't abandon me, and now, I can be sure of it." And he could feel Rikar in the back of his mind.

He was still trying to get used to it, but it was reassuring. At any moment, if he needed to leave, he just had to say the word without even taking his phone out, and Rikar would come for him.

Rikar would always come for him.

Since Rikar had told Hayes he'd be telling his mothers about him and Samara, he had to do it. He wasn't looking forward to it, not because he was afraid their reaction would be bad, but rather, the opposite.

They'd be over the moon happy for him because he'd found his mate and had bonded with him and because of Samara. That was what would make them the happiest. They'd wanted grandchildren for a while now, and with Samara in their life, they'd get that. Rikar wondered if he'd ever see Samara again once his mothers got their hands on her, but he supposed he was about to find out.

"Ready to go?" he asked.

Samara shuffled her feet. She still wasn't wearing her

shoes, even though Rikar told her to put them on what felt like a dozen times.

It probably had been more.

"What if they don't like me?" Samara asked.

It was tempting to brush off her fear and reassure her that they'd love her, but Rikar didn't want to do that. It was a legitimate fear, and while he knew his mothers would love Samara, eventually, she'd meet someone who didn't like her. She'd have to learn to deal with that, which wouldn't be easy. She'd never had many people in her life and needed love and affection, but she wouldn't get it from everyone.

"Then they don't like you. It won't change anything—not that I'm going to adopt you or that Hayes and I love you."

"But they could ask you not to adopt me anymore."

"They could, but it's not the kind of people they are. Even if they did, though, it wouldn't change my decision. I made you a promise, and I'll keep it because I want to and it's the right thing to do."

She bit her lower lip. Rikar had braided her hair, so it was away from her face for once. She liked to hide behind it, but Rikar had come to realize it was a way for her to ignore the world. She had to stop doing that, no matter how hard it was. The first step was braiding hair, but hopefully, it wouldn't be the last.

"I don't want you to fight with them because of me," she eventually said.

"Even if I do fight with them, it wouldn't be because of you, but rather, because of them and their reaction to you. I love my mothers, but I wouldn't want to have a relationship with someone who can't see how important it is for me to adopt you." Rikar sighed and squeezed one of Samara's shoulders. "But I promise you that they're going to love you. I understand why you're so hesitant and afraid, and it's all right to feel that way. I'd be worried if you didn't, to be honest. You don't have anything to worry about when it comes to my mothers. Even if they don't like you, they'll accept my decision. Besides, I'm an adult, aren't I? It's not like they can put me in timeout anymore."

Samara giggled. "I'm too old to be put in timeout, too."

"I don't know about that." Maybe she was. She was already ten, and it wasn't like Rikar had any experience dealing with a ten-year-old. He wouldn't know where to start if they had to punish her, and while he knew he might have to eventually, he hoped it wouldn't happen anytime soon. It would break his heart to take anything away from Samara or to put her in a corner or however that worked.

"Now, are you ready to go?" he asked again.

This time, she nodded and finally grabbed her shoes. It took her way too long to put them on and do the laces, but eventually, they were ready. Rikar pulled Samara's hat lower, made sure her coat was zipped up, and guided her out of the house.

He loved living in town, and not just because it was where his tribe lived. His home wasn't far from Main Street, but it was far enough away that he had privacy. It still only took him and Samara a few minutes to reach the diner, where once again, he was meeting his mothers.

He hoped there would be no blind date this time.

What had happened the last time he'd met them here was still fresh in his mind. It hadn't been entirely their fault, or rather, it had been, but he understood why they'd organized a blind date. He didn't need one anymore, though. He had Hayes, and they were bonded.

Hayes didn't often communicate with Rikar through their bond. He probably wasn't used to being able to do so yet, and while Rikar couldn't wait for a time in which he was, he also enjoyed feeling Hayes in the back of his mind. Even now, he could tell that while Hayes was a little worried, he was also happy to be with his mother. He felt at peace, and in the end, that was all that mattered when it came to family. Hayes's mother had only wanted the best for him, just like Rikar's mothers did for him. They'd gone about it the wrong way, but everything was fine now, or at least, Rikar thought so.

When he and Samara reached the diner, he peeked through the window. He was relieved to see that his mothers were alone this time, their heads close together as they talked. Edna was gesturing, while Blodwyn nodded at whatever she was saying.

Edna was the chatty type. She was a troublemaker, always playing with Rikar when he was a child, daring him to do things that got both of them in trouble. Blodwyn, on the other hand, was more down-to-earth. Rikar enjoyed watching movies and reading with her, and she'd always been who he went to when he had trouble with school. They were different, but Rikar wouldn't have it any other way. He loved both of them equally, and that would never change.

He pushed open the diner door and walked in. Samara grabbed his hand and clutched it, and he was more than happy to let her do so. He guided her toward the table at the back of the diner, and of course, his mothers noticed them before he was ready for them to.

Edna's eyes widened, and she scrambled to get to her feet while Blodwyn stayed where she was and put a hand on Edna's arm. Edna said something, but Blodwyn shook her head and pulled her back down.

Rikar was glad Blodwyn was there. He wasn't sure he would have been able to deal with Edna and Samara on his own.

"I'm glad to see there's no surprise tonight," he said when he reached them.

"You were clear that you didn't want any more blind dates, so I made sure your mother didn't find you someone else,"

Blodwyn said. Her gaze was on Samara, though.

Rikar kissed her cheek, then turned to Edna. "I'm surprised you listened."

She huffed. "I was tempted not to, but Blodwyn said that you might stop talking to me if I continued pushing you, and I wasn't about to risk that. Now, who's this little girl? Is she one of the children who were rescued from the lab?"

Rikar wasn't surprised his mother had heard about the lab. The entire town had by now, which made sense since he'd had to place several children in homes that belonged to tribe members. Not everyone who lived in town was a tribe member, but even those who weren't worked closely with the tribe and its members.

Rikar put his hands on Samara's shoulders. "This is Samara. Yes, she's one of the children the mutants found in that last lab, and Hayes and I are in the process of adopting her."

Edna screeched, startling both Samara and Rikar, but Blodwyn kept her cool, at least for now. Her eyes narrowed, and she turned her attention to Rikar. "Who is Hayes? One of the mutants?"

"He is. He's also my mate, and we're bonded."

This time, Blodwyn screeched, too. She and Edna got so loud that half the people in the diner turned to look at them. Rikar didn't care. They were reacting this way because they cared about him and were happy for him, and now that they were focused on him, it gave Samara a few seconds to breathe.

Edna grabbed Rikar's arm and pulled him down next to her. "You met your mate? Why didn't you tell us? When did you meet him? When did you bond? When are we meeting him?"

Rikar grinned. "It would be easier to tell you what happened if you let me talk."

Edna mimed locking her lips and throwing away the key. She also winked at Samara, who giggled.

Rikar relaxed. He hadn't been worried about his mothers reaction to Samara, and he hoped that now that she'd met them, Samara felt better about it, too. It would take time for her to get used to being part of the family, but now that she was with them and away from the lab, time wouldn't be a problem.

It would never be a problem again.

Hayes had never told his mother exactly what he'd been through in the lab. He hadn't wanted to hurt or scare her, but he realized that maybe he should have. It would have made his experience more real to her, and she might have better understood why he couldn't stay back and let someone else help the people who were still stuck in cages.

So this time, he told her. He still didn't go into details because he didn't think he could stand it, but he made sure she understood how much pain he had hidden and how terrified he'd been. By the time he was done, her eyes were wide and red, and she was crying. She'd grabbed one of his hands partway through his explanation and squeezed it almost hard enough to break it.

Hayes gave her a sad smile. "So, you understand why I have to do this now? I can't let anyone go through that if I can avoid it, especially children."

His mother wiped her tears with her free hand. She didn't let go of him, almost as if she were afraid that if she did, he'd vanish.

"I'd say I can't believe a human being would do something like that, but by now, I've heard enough stories that I *can* believe it, unfortunately," she said.

Hayes nodded. "In that lab, I learned how awful humans can be to each other. I promise I'll be careful and won't put myself in danger without reason, but I need to do this."

His mother stared at him for a moment before nodding. "I won't try to stop you anymore, but you do realize that what happened wasn't your fault, right? You were kidnapped and tortured. That all lies on the shoulders of the people who took you, not on you. Even if you decided that you can't deal with this anymore, whatever happens to the people still in those cages won't be your fault, either."

Hayes gave his mother a crooked smile. "My therapist says it's survivor's guilt. I survived and made it out of the lab, but some of the people I was in there with didn't. Some of the people my friends and I have found in other labs were dead, too." A few of the kids they'd found in the last lab hadn't made it, but Hayes couldn't think of that without wanting to cry. "She warned me that pushing myself too hard and too far might hurt me, but I don't know what else to do."

"Well, you could focus on that mate of yours and your daughter."

Hayes's smile widened. He had a daughter now. He had a mate, and while he could hardly believe it, he found himself reaching for Rikar in the back of his mind.

He knew he could talk to Rikar, but he didn't. It was enough for him to feel his mate. Rikar was warm and gentle, like spring sunshine on Hayes's skin. He'd always be there, whether Hayes needed him or not.

"*That* is why I wanted you to come home so badly," Hayes's mother said, pointing her finger at him.

"I'm not sure what you're talking about."

"That smile. I hadn't seen it since before you were taken."

Hayes touched a fingertip to his lower lip. "I didn't have many reasons to smile before."

"And I was trying to give you back those reasons. I'll admit I shouldn't have meddled so much and that I shouldn't have pushed, but I only wanted you to be happy. I thought I could help you with that."

"And you can, just not by asking my ex-boyfriend to come over for dinner."

"You and Benedict were good together."

"We were, and I'll always cherish the memories of our time together. But I'm not the same person I was when I was kidnapped."

His mother's smile vanished. "I suppose you're not. No one would be after what you've been through." She squeezed his hand harder. "I'm proud of you, Hayes. So many people would have broken down after what you've gone through, but you didn't. Instead, you're doing everything you can to help people, even though you might get hurt. I'm terrified of losing you again, but I won't try to stop you. I understand better why you have to do this now, and I'd never forgive myself if I lost my relationship with you because I'm too stubborn to realize that I don't have a say in your life anymore. Just remember that whenever you need me, I'll be here, ready to help."

Hayes felt like he was about to cry. "I'd be careful about that promise. I might take you up on it and have you babysit Samara."

"I'd be delighted. She's my first granddaughter, and I've already lost enough time with her. I hate that she had to spend so many years in the foster system."

"So do I, but she's with us now."

"When can I see them?"

"Soon, I hope. Rikar is pretty busy, but I'm sure he can make some time."

Hayes's mother finally let go of his hand and took a sip of her tea. It had to be cold by now, and she grimaced and put the mug down.

"I need to apologize to Rikar," she said.

"You can, but it's not necessary. He understands you were only trying to help me."

"It still doesn't make the way I treated him right. I shouldn't have been so cold. It was rude of me, and I wish to fix that."

"Why were you? I thought you'd be happy to find out that I had a mate."

"And I am. I was the other evening, too."

"It didn't seem like it."

Hayes's mother sighed. "I was afraid. I still am. As I told you before, I've only wanted you and your brother to be happy. When you disappeared, I thought I'd lost you, and when you came back, I told myself I'd do everything I could to make sure you stayed with me. You had a whole other life, but I felt like if you didn't come home, I might lose you again."

Hayes had thought about that. He'd been terrified and in pain in the lab, but since he'd come back, he'd also thought about how his family had taken his kidnapping. He knew how he'd feel and react if Lucas were to disappear, so he couldn't blame his mother for trying to pull him back into the fold and never letting go. He'd probably do the same with Samara if he lost her. He'd *definitely* do the same with Rikar.

It was logical to want to cling on after losing someone, then getting them back. At least Hayes's mother realized that she'd done this the wrong way and that there were better ways to get Hayes to go back home.

"I don't think I'll ever be moving back, but it doesn't mean I won't visit," he told his mother. "I promise that I'm careful when it comes to the labs. It's not like we raid one every week, anyway. It takes a lot of time and effort to find out where they are, hack into databases, and get all the information we need. But if it makes you feel better, I can promise to let you know every time we find one."

Hayes wasn't surprised when his mother shook her head. "I don't want to know," she said. "I'd freak out, here at home, knowing you're in a fight. But if you ever need anything after the attacks, even if it's only a place for some of the people you rescue to rest, then call me. I want to help."

"You don't have to."

"Maybe not, but you were right when you said that you'd never forgive yourself if you looked the other way and didn't do what you could to help the people still going through that. You were lucky. Someone got you out and took care of you. Now, it's our turn to do so."

Hayes and his family were in this together, and he was glad for that. For a few days, he'd thought he'd lost his mother. But Rikar had pushed him to come back to talk to her, and she'd seen the light.

Hayes was happy, and she could see that. She could see that he didn't need anything more than what he already had.

A mate, a home, and a daughter.

Rikar was relieved when Hayes finally contacted him.

Hey, can you pick me up? Hayes asked.

Rikar found himself smiling. *Of course. You're still with your mother?*

Yeah. We had a talk, and things are much better.

Rikar was relieved. He'd hoped Hayes's mother would eventually understand where Hayes was coming from and why he didn't want to move home. He'd been terrified that Hayes would lose his parents, but it looked like they'd fixed things.

Samara and I will be there right away.

Fair warning. My mother wants to talk to you and apologize. I'm also pretty sure she might try to steal Samara away from us if we're not careful.

Rikar smiled. This was all he'd ever wanted in his life, and he had it. It might be more complicated than he'd expected, but he wasn't afraid of complications and hard work. Besides,

Samara deserved a grandmother who doted on her. She already had two, as Rikar had found out at the diner, but a third one would be welcome, too.

We'll be there as soon as possible. Give us a few minutes to ditch my mothers.

The sound of Hayes's laughter filled Rikar's mind. He couldn't remember a life without Hayes and Samara in it, and he hoped he'd never have to go back to it.

It wasn't easy to extricate Samara from the loving hands of Rikar's mothers. He only managed by telling them that they needed to pick up Hayes and promising they could all have dinner together soon. He'd have to talk to Hayes first, but he thought his mate would be up to meeting his mothers. They couldn't wait, and while Rikar knew it would be intimidating for Hayes, he wanted their families to blend and for everyone to get along.

As soon as Rikar's mothers let go of Samara, Rikar grabbed her and shimmered her away. They landed on the porch of the house where Hayes's parents lived, and the door flew open instantly. Hayes stood there, a smile on his face, a bit huffy. "My mother wants to meet Samara."

Rikar looked down at the girl. "What do you think? Want to meet another grandmother?"

This time, Samara was more enthusiastic about it. She nodded, and when Hayes offered her his hand, she took it easily. She was still careful as she followed him into the house, Rikar right behind them, but there was nothing for her or Rikar and Hayes to worry about.

Hayes's mother was in the kitchen. She smiled when she saw Samara, and Rikar knew everything would be okay.

Hayes leaned against Rikar's side, and Rikar wrapped an arm around him as they both watched Samara and his mother.

"She wants to apologize," Hayes said.

"She doesn't need to. Besides, this is the best apology I

could have hoped for. She seems happy to have Samara in her life."

"That's because she is. She's already told me that Samara is her first grandchild and that she wants to spend as much time as possible with her since they didn't have the opportunity to do so while Samara was younger."

"That would have been hard considering we just met her. But I don't have a problem with them spending time together. We'll probably be happy to have your mother once Samara comes out of her shell."

Hayes nodded. "What about yours? How did they react to the news?"

"They were happy. In the end, that was all the three of them wanted for us, wasn't it?"

Hayes nodded. "I could have done without both of us having to go on a blind date, though."

Rikar laughed. "Well, we got two friends out of those. It can't be bad."

"It's not."

They watched Samara interact with Hayes's mother for a moment before Hayes asked, "I've been meaning to ask, but have you already started the documents and everything to make the adoption official?"

"I have. Your brother is working with the council, and they're making things as easy as possible." Rikar hesitated. He'd wanted to talk about this for a while now, but he was afraid it was too soon and too much for Hayes. Still, he wouldn't know if he didn't at least throw it out there. "I've asked your brother to put your name on the adoption papers, too. We can get rid of it if you're not ready, but I think it would be important for Samara to have two parents. Not that you're not already a parent to her since we're raising her together, but I'd like for it to be official, and I think she would, too. I don't want her to wonder why you haven't adopted her while I have."

Hayes's smile was soft. "You can stop panicking. I'd be happy to have my name next to yours on her application. Besides, now that we're bonded, it goes without saying."

Rikar kissed the top of Hayes's head. "It probably does for many people, but I just want to be sure that everything is perfect." Rikar didn't want to risk someone coming to him and trying to take Samara back. He had no way to know where Samara's mother was or if she ever would try to find her daughter again. If she did, he'd make sure Samara had a choice. She wouldn't be forced to go back with the mother who had abandoned her when she'd needed her.

"I think we'll be okay," Hayes whispered.

"I think we will, too."

Their future wouldn't be perfect, and it wouldn't be easy. Both Hayes and Samara were dealing with PTSD and other consequences of what had been done to them in the labs. Sometimes, Rikar wasn't sure there was enough of him to take care of both of them, but he wouldn't have it any other way. They were both seeing a therapist, and Rikar had started to wonder if maybe he should, too. Sometimes, dealing with so many nightmares and the knowledge of what had been done to the people he loved weighed heavily on his shoulders and his mind.

Hayes and Samara would always be his priorities, though. Finding his own therapist could wait until he was sure they'd both settled in their new life. Once he'd taken care of them, he could take care of himself.

Something touched the tip of his nose, making him jerk back. Hayes laughed. His hand was still raised.

"You were deep in thought," he said.

"I was just thinking about the future."

Hayes stared at him for a moment before nodding. "I often think about the future, too. I'm glad it'll be with you."

"As am I. I couldn't think of a better mate than you."

"And even if you could, you're stuck with me." Hayes's expression turned serious. "But I want you to know that I'll take care of you and Samara."

"I already know that."

"I realize I have a lot to work on, and I will. Just, please, can you promise that you'll tell me if there's anything wrong or anything that makes you unhappy? I don't want things to fester between us."

"I promise I'll tell you if there's anything wrong." Rikar had no doubt that something would be eventually, but it would be part of the challenges of their lives. They'd face them together, just like they had until now, and they'd win.

Rikar wouldn't have it any other way.

Samara ran to them, and Rikar let go of Hayes's shoulders to grab her. She was still too light for a ten-year-old, and he was able to haul her up into his arms. "Ready to go home?" he asked.

Samara nodded. "She told me to call her grandma."

"Then that's what you should call her, if you're all right with that."

"I've never had a grandmother, and now, I have three."

And they'd love Samara the way only grandmothers could. Even if something happened to Rikar and Hayes, it wouldn't be the end for Samara.

But nothing would happen to them. They were starting their life together, surrounded by love and happiness, and it was almost as if every single one of Rikar's dreams had come true.

CHAPTER SEVEN

Hayes rushed through the kitchen, needing to make sure everything was perfect. The turkey was roasting in the oven, and the kitchen looked like something had exploded right on the counter. There was food everywhere, along with every single bowl Hayes had been able to find in the house.

"You do realize this is only a family dinner, right?" Lucas asked from the kitchen door.

Hayes glared at him. "If you don't have anything useful to say, you know where the door is."

But instead of leaving, Lucas stepped in. "Again. This isn't Thanksgiving dinner. We're having that one at Mom and Dad's."

"I'm very much aware of that." Thanksgiving was still more than a month away, and considering how much work this dinner had been, Hayes was glad his parents had offered to host that one.

He still wanted this dinner to be perfect.

It was the first time his and Rikar's family would meet. The past few months had been a whirlwind of getting used to living with Samara and Rikar and settling down as a family. Samara had started school, albeit reluctantly, and she was doing well. Hayes had taken a step back from raiding the labs so he could stay with Samara and not risk her freaking out when he left, but eventually, he'd go back. He still had a lot to offer, and he wanted to make sure not even one person was left in one of those cages. For now, though, his family took precedent, as was right.

The problem was that his family also made him nuts. He hadn't realized he'd freak out so badly when he'd invited both his parents and Rikar's for dinner. He'd called it a trial Thanksgiving dinner, and he still remembered how skeptical his mother had been. Hayes had never hosted a Thanksgiving dinner, and while he'd watched his mother prepare many of them over the years, he'd never realized how much work was behind them.

Now, he did.

"Do you need help?" Lucas asked.

"Not really. I have everything under control."

Lucas arched a brow and looked around the room. "Do you?"

Hayes huffed and went to the sink to wash his hands. "I promise I do. All the food is ready to go on the table, at least once the turkey is. It won't be long, so you can go back to the living room."

"I'm fine here. I mean, it was fun to watch Mom ask Rikar's mothers questions and be bewildered by Edna's answers, but I wanted to check in on you."

Hayes stopped moving and sucked in a breath. "I told you that I'm fine."

"I'm not talking about the dinner, although you really should calm down. I want to know about everything else. There have been a lot of changes in your life lately, and I know it can be overwhelming."

It was. Hayes wasn't sure what he'd have done without his therapist, but thankfully, he didn't have to find out. She'd been there for him every step of the way and would continue being there until he didn't need her anymore. Right now, it felt impossible for him to stand on his own two feet, but that was fine.

He didn't have to.

He had precious and important people in his life, like

Samara and Rikar, but they weren't his only support system. He had his parents, his brother, and the other mutants. They were all happy that he'd found his mate and that he was building a life. He supposed it made sense. It gave them hope that they'd find someone, too, eventually.

Hayes wanted them to.

He wanted every single one of them to find happiness, whatever it meant for them. What they were doing with the labs and saving people was good, but it couldn't be their entire lives. They needed more, and to remember that even after what happened to them, they'd survived.

Sometimes, Hayes had a hard time remembering that. It only took one touch from Rikar, one word from Samara, and he did. They might not be his entire life, but they were his heart.

"There you are," Hayes's mother said as she walked into the kitchen.

Hayes and Lucas exchanged a glance. Lucas started to retreat toward the door, but Hayes grabbed his wrist and pulled him back, then grinned a smile that had to look fake at their mother. "Do you need anything?"

She frowned when she looked at him. "Do you need to go to the bathroom?"

"Definitely not. Why?"

"Your face. It looks like you need to go to the bathroom. You can. I'll keep an eye on the turkey."

"I'm fine." Hayes let go of Lucas, who rushed toward the door — the traitor. "I told you I'd be hosting, and it's still the plan."

"It doesn't mean you have to do everything on your own."

"I'm not. Rikar helped me a lot in the beginning."

"And I kept him away after I arrived. I'm sorry."

Hayes's mother had been apologizing a lot since they'd made peace, and no matter how many times he told her she needed to stop, she didn't seem to be able to. He hoped that in time, she'd realize he wasn't angry at her for how she'd behaved.

"Did I hear my name?" Rikar asked. He walked into the kitchen, his gaze twinkling. "Samara was looking for you," he told Hayes's mother.

She beamed. "Let me see what she wants. I'll be right back to help," she promised.

"I don't need help," Hayes called after her.

He wasn't sure if she'd heard or listened to him, but that was okay. He leaned back against the counter and took a deep breath. He needed to keep it together until it was over.

He closed his eyes and smiled when he felt fingertips dancing along his cheekbone. "What are you doing?" he asked without opening his eyes.

"You look tired."

"Thanks for the compliment."

"You're beautiful, like always, but you also looked tired. You should have let me do more for this dinner."

Hayes shouldn't have organized this dinner, to begin with, but he wasn't about to say that out loud. Instead, he pushed away from the counter and into Rikar's arms.

Rikar welcomed him easily. They fit together like they were made for each other, and it gave Hayes peace to know that they were. He didn't care who had made the decision, just that he was happy with Rikar in his life. Adding Samara to the mix meant that sometimes, Hayes was afraid of losing everything because of how much he had, but it was becoming easier to dismiss those fears.

He'd never have his life taken away from him again. Rikar would make sure of that, and Hayes trusted him. He'd never trusted anyone as much as he trusted Rikar.

Rikar wrapped his arms around Hayes and held him close. He ran his lips along Hayes's forehead in tiny kisses, then kissed the top of his head. "All right?" he asked.

Hayes nodded. "Better now that you're here, though."

"It doesn't matter if I've already helped you. I can help again."

"That would be great. Honestly, I'm not looking forward to doing the dishes."

"We'll think about that later. Right now, you need to focus on your family and nothing else."

Hayes could hear the sound of people talking in the other room. The voices mixed, both male and female, and under them was the sound of a young girl laughing. Even if Hayes didn't save one more person in his entire life, he'd saved Samara.

And that was more than enough to make him feel satisfied with the choices he'd made and the life he lived.

ABOUT THE AUTHOR

Catherine is the creator of several series, most of them paranormal, including the Whitedell Pride Series and the Gillham Pack Series. While she graduated in translation, she decided to go the writer's way because it was more fun to create her own stories and characters.

She's been living in Italy for more than twenty years, but she's a daughter of the North—Belgium to be precise—and she misses it so much that she's already planning to move back.

She loves pizza—probably too much—her son, her pets, and of course, books. She sneaks some reading time into her schedule every time she has five minutes free from writing, demands from her various pets and son, and lastly, housework.

Connect with her:

lievens.catherine@gmail.com
BookBub: https://www.bookbub.com/authors/catherine-lievens
Website: https://authorcatherinelievens.com/
Facebook: https://www.facebook.com/catherine.lievens.9
Facebook Group: https://www.facebook.com/groups/411788002341528/
Twitter: https://twitter.com/authorCLievens
Newsletter: http://eepurl.com/c-uvKn